THE ELEPHANT'S BATHTUB

FRANCES CARPENTER

The Elephant's Bathtub

WONDER TALES
FROM THE FAR EAST

Illustrated by Hans Guggenheim

Doubleday & Company, Inc., Garden City, New York

Library of Congress Catalog Card Number 62–16499
Designed by Pete Landa
Title Page Calligraphy by Joe Ascherl
Printed in the United States of America
First Edition

ACKNOWLEDGMENTS

The themes of the ancient folktales in this book have been collected by the author from many sources. Among these, special mention should be made of the following:

Contes Birmans d'après le Thoudamma Sari Dammazat, Louis Vossion, 1901; *Contes Populaires du Cambodge, du Laos, et du Siam,* Auguste Pavie, 1903; *Contes Cambodgiens,* Adhemard et Leclere, 1903; *Laos Folklore of Farther India,* Katherine N. Fleeson, 1899; *Studies of Religion, Folklore, and Customs in British North Borneo and the Malay Peninsula,* Ivor H. N. Evans, 1923; *Folk Tales of Iraq,* E. S. Stevens (Drower) 1931; *Les Contes Fantastiques du Vietnam,* Con Hô' Miêu; *Epics, Myths, and Legends of India,* F. Thomas; *Myths and Symbols in Indian Art,* Heinrich Zimmer, 1946; *Folk Tales of Kashmir,* Rev. J. Hinton Knowles, 1893; *Buddhist Legends,* G. de Vasconcellos-Abreu, trans. from the Portuguese by Donald Ferguson, 1880; *The Travels of Fâ Hien,* James Legge; *Persian Legends Retold,* Youel B. Mirza, 1935; *Village Folk Tales of Ceylon,* H. Parker, 1914; *Mahavansa, Great Chronicle of Ceylon,* trans. William Geiger, 1908; *Tales of Fish and People of the Ceylon Estuary,* J. A. R. Grenier; *Traditions of the Tinguian, A Study in Philippine Folklore,* Fay-Cooper Cole, 1915; *Filipino Popular Tales,* Dean S. Fansler, American Folklore Society, 1921; *Tales of Long Ago in the Philippines,* Maximo Ramos; *Bannu, Our Afghan Frontier,* S. S. Thorburn, 1876; and *The Romance of the Harem,* Anna Leonowens, 1873.

CONTENTS

THE ELEPHANT'S BATHTUB

THE ELEPHANT'S BATHTUB

Long ago—oh, very long ago—on the other side of the world, there was a Burmese King named Mindo Min. He was a good King. But he was not very bright, as this story will prove.

In Burma, in those times, a King was important. A golden umbrella was always held over his head. Not only when he walked in the royal gardens in the hot sun, but also when he sat on his shining throne, inside his splendid palace, there was this golden umbrella. It was a sign of his majesty.

An even clearer sign of a Burmese King's importance was the elephant upon which he rode when he came out of the palace gates.

"Lord of One Thousand Elephants!" So the Burmese people saluted their King. And they bowed their heads down to touch the ground before his magnificent beast.

Of course, Mindo Min did not have, actually, one thousand

elephants. But no doubt he had many, for the jungles of Burma were the home of great herds of these huge beasts. His elephants were more important to this King than his golden throne, his gem-studded crown with its tall point, and his golden umbrella.

Elephants were the greatest treasures of any King in Southeast Asia. Especially important it was that he should have in his palace stables a white elephant. These rare beasts were said to have come to earth straight from the Sky-World. They were thought to be able to bring rain out of the clouds when it was needed for the rice fields.

Alas, there was not even one white elephant among the beasts in Mindo Min's stables. It made him sick with jealousy each time he thought of his neighbor, the King of Siam. This King had so many that his country was known far and wide as the "Land of White Elephants."

Bags full of gold coins were kept ready for that jungle hunter who might bring Mindo Min one of these pale-gray beasts with the pinkish spots on their flapping ears and their long trunks. You see, these Far Eastern "white elephants" are not actually white. Their hides are only a little bit lighter than those of their ordinary darker-gray brothers.

This story is about Mindo Min's wish to own a white elephant. But it tells also of another man, who was not at all important like Mindo Min. This man was like the great Burmese King only in that he, too, was jealous of a luckier neighbor.

The other jealous man was a potmaker. Po Bah was his name, and he lived on the banks of a river that ran through Mindo Min's city. In those long-ago times, the people of Burma bought their cups and their pots, their eating bowls, their great water jars, and their washing tubs from potmakers like Po Bah.

Po Bah made fine bowls and tubs. When he spread his wares out in the marketplace, many came to buy them. So he should have been happy. He should have been content with his comfortable house, his good wife, and his children.

He might have been happy, perhaps, if his next-door neighbor, Saw Ka, the washerman, had not had a better house. As Po Bah used the clay on the banks of the river for making his pots, so Saw Ka used its water to wash all kinds of things clean. The river was the reason why both of these men had built their houses so near it.

Everyone said Po Bah made the best pots in the city. They said also that Saw Ka was the very best washerman. Out of his tubs came clothes as white as the very clouds in the sky. From morning until night the washerman worked hard. And he became rich.

Po Bah could have been just as rich, if he had worked just as hard. But he was too jealous. For thinking about the good fortune of his neighbor, he could hardly dig enough clay to make the pots and the tubs he needed to sell.

"I must think of some way to spoil the luck of Saw Ka," the unhappy potmaker said to himself at last. He thought and thought. And then he made a plan.

"Our neighbor will not be so rich when I am through with him," the potmaker said to his wife one day. She, too, was jealous. Saw Ka's wife had a finer silk jacket than hers. She had a more costly gold necklace. And she wore a real ruby button in one side of her nose. So Po Bah's wife did not try to keep her jealous husband from going on with the mean trick he planned to play on his neighbor.

It was to the King, Mindo Min, that Po Bah went with his plan.

"Lord of One Thousand Elephants!" The potmaker crawled on his knees to the foot of the golden throne under the shining umbrella. "O Lord of the Sun, Child of the Moon, your people are sad that you do not have a white elephant. Your jungle hunters are truly unlucky. But I have thought of a way in which such a heavenly beast may be yours."

"Speak then, Potmaker!" Mindo Min's tawny face brightened. He could already see himself mounted upon the "white elephant," with its pale, mouse-colored hide and the many pink spots on its ears and its trunk.

"Well, my neighbor Saw Ka, the washerman, makes magic on the banks of our river. Clothes quite as dark as the gray hide of an elephant come out of his tubs as white as a summer cloud. Why should he not make such magic on one of your gray elephants? Let him whiten the beast. Thus Mindo Min may truly be called 'Lord of the White Elephant.'"

The jealous potmaker was happy when he saw the King's smile. He thought to himself, "When the washerman cannot do as he commands, the King will be angry. He will send Saw Ka far away into the northern mountains. Then I shall not have to watch him grow richer and richer." These were, indeed, his wicked thoughts.

That foolish King called Saw Ka, the washerman, to come to his palace.

"I command you, Saw Ka, to wash my largest gray elephant white," Mindo Min cried out in a loud voice. "When you have done that, you shall have two bags of gold."

"Ha! Ha! Ho! Ho!" This was a good joke. Everyone in that

throne room burst into laughter. The one who laughed loudest was, of course, that mean man, Po Bah.

The washerman was just about to laugh himself. But he saw the King's face grow dark. And he heard him say, "Saw Ka, if you do not wash my elephant white, you shall be sent to the northern mountains."

So Saw Ka did not laugh. When he saw the broad grin on the face of Po Bah, he knew that his jealous neighbor was the one who had set this trap for him.

"Son of the Sun, O Child of the Moon"—he bowed his head down to touch the ground—"with all my skill I will try to obey your command.

"The Lord of All Elephants knows, I am sure"—Saw Ka had to think quickly—"that a washerman cannot work without a tub. What is to be made white must be given a bath with soap in warm water. Now, alas, I do not have a tub large enough to hold an elephant. But that is no great matter. My good neighbor, Po Bah, the potmaker can easily make such a tub. As soon as he has ready a bathtub for your elephant, I will try to wash it white."

The palace people hid their smiles behind their hands. They knew it would be as impossible to make a bathtub for an elephant as it would be to change the color of its hide.

Their foolish King, however, was nodding his head. This washerman spoke well. Making a bathtub, everyone knew, was the work of a man who made things out of clay.

"Potmaker," cried Mindo Min. "You shall make me a bathtub that will hold my largest elephant. Make it at once so that the washerman can begin his work."

"Why does not the washerman give the elephant a bath down

in the river?" Po Bah saw that he was about to be caught in his own trap.

"The flowing water would carry my soapsuds away," Saw Ka replied. Now it was his turn to smile. "River water is cool. A good bath in warm soapy water will be needed to wash the King's elephant white."

The potmaker's face fell. What could he do now? He would never dare tell the King his plan was only a trick.

"I never have made so large a tub. But I will try," he said at last.

Po Bah called his friends and his family to help him gather the clay. All working together, they shaped it into a tub. Big it was, truly, big enough for an elephant. It took twenty men to help Po Bah carry that tub to the palace.

"Well done, Potmaker!" cried Mindo Min. "Now bring out the beast," the King called to the elephant's keeper.

The huge tub was filled. A fire was made around it to warm the water inside it. Soap was put in and stirred to make thick foamy suds.

"Lift!" the elephant's keeper called to the beast. One huge gray foot was set down inside the tub. And at once there was a crash. The clay tub was broken into a thousand pieces. The soapy water flew out in every direction. It even spattered the silken robes of the King, who was watching, close by, under his golden umbrella.

"Your tub was not strong enough, Potmaker!" There was anger in Mindo Min's voice. "Make another tub, and stronger, so that it shall not break."

So again the friends and the family of Po Bah set to work. Their next tub was so strong that it did not even crack when the elephant put all his four feet inside it. But its bottom was so thick that the heat of the fire around it could not reach the water.

"Without warm water, O Mindo Min, the elephant truly cannot be washed white." Again Saw Ka could smile.

"Then Po Bah shall make us still another tub, with a bottom that is neither too thick nor too thin." The King was determined that he should have his white elephant.

Again, and yet again, that poor potmaker tried to make a bathtub for the King's elephant. But it was always the same story. If the bottom was thin so that its water could be warmed, the tub broke into bits under the elephant's weight. If it was thick enough to hold the beast, the water remained cool.

No one knows what would have happened to that poor, jealous potmaker if the King's hunters had not, just then, found a real white elephant in the Burmese jungle. Of light mouse color it was. There were splendid pink patches on its ears and its trunk. And each of its great feet had five toes instead of only four.

In his joy, Mindo Min called for a feast which lasted a month. In choosing a name and in christening his gift from the Sky-World, he quite forgot about washing the other gray elephant white.

The jealous potmaker, however, was not yet out of trouble. For weeks he had spent all his time on the elephant's bathtub.

Not one pot or bowl—not even a cup—had he made to sell in the marketplace. He had spent all his money. There was no food in his house. His children were hungry.

It was then that his neighbor, Saw Ka, showed his good heart. He brought a huge basket, filled with rice, to the house next door.

"I bear you no ill will, Po Bah," he said, "though you did try to ruin me. You should not blame me that you are now in such a sad plight. Is it my fault that I work harder than you? Each of us must live and work as he likes. So let us be friends."

What happened then? Who knows? It was so long ago.

Did the potmaker forget his jealousy? Did the two neighbors thereafter live side by side in peace?

However it was, surely that potmaker and that washerman both said prayers for the health of the King's real white elephant. Surely neither one wanted to hear ever again the words "elephant's bathtub."

THE FISH WITH BENT NOSES

In the faraway Asian land of Cambodia, the Big Rains come always at the same time of year. Then the fishermen spread their nets out across the wide Mekong River.

They keep watch for the strange fish which they call the "Ones with Bent Noses." For it is with the Big Rains that these "bent-nosed ones" swim in from the South China Sea. By the hundreds they come; yes, by the thousands they crowd their way up the river.

That is when the Cambodian grandmothers say to the children, "The Fish with Bent Noses are trying once more to reach the temple of the Great Buddha. But our fishermen will stop them. They will take so many into their nets that we shall have food for many moons."

"Why do the Fish with Bent Noses want to go to the temple of Buddha, Grandmother?" The children always ask this question.

"They want to ask pardon for the wicked deed of their

forefather who was a thief. Because of that fish-thief, bad luck came to these fish. It was because of him, too, that their noses turn down."

Then the Cambodian grandmothers tell this story, just as it is set down here for you.

Long ago, in this land, there lived a good Prince whose name was Sotat. He was young. He was kind. And, oh, he was handsome. With his big eyes and full lips, Prince Sotat was as noble to look upon as any of the stone gods in the temple at Angkor Wat.

Some say this good Prince was in truth a Holy One. But however that may have been, he was beloved by Buddha, as you shall see.

One fine day when Sotat was traveling in a neighboring kingdom, he came to a brook. He was thirsty, and so he stopped for a drink of its crystal-clear water. He was just shaping a large green leaf into a cup when a young girl came down the path along the edge of the brook. On her head she was carrying a tall water jar.

"Good day," said the Prince in his warm, friendly way. "Will you be so kind as to give me a drink from your water jar? My throat is dry from the heat and dust of the highroad."

"Gladly, good Sir. I have plenty of water, and I can dip up more from the brook." The girl bowed politely.

"Where do you go with your water, my Child?" Sotat asked.

"To the King's palace." She pointed to tall shining towers which could be seen through the trees. "I am bringing fresh water to cool the head of my mistress, the Princess Keo Fa."

"Everyone says your Princess is beautiful and good as well."

Prince Sotat had already heard high praise for the fair daughter of the King of this land.

"Indeed, my lady is beautiful and as good as an angel. There is no Princess like her in all the world." The palace maid's eyes were shining with love for her lady.

When Sotat heard her glowing words, his heart was touched. "Why should I not wed this fair Princess? If she is so fair and so good, I could love her well." Of course, he said no word of his thought aloud. But it was as if the girl had seen into his heart.

"Everyone loves Keo Fa," she said. "Her father loves her so dearly that we do not think he will ever give her up to a bridegroom. His heart would be broken if some handsome Prince should carry her away with him to another land."

Sotat lifted her water jar and he drank. Then he handed it back to her.

When the maid returned to the palace, she told her Princess about the noble young man she had met by the brook.

"He is like a young god, dear Lady. Goodness shines from his eyes. You should have heard his sweet thanks when he had drunk from my jar."

As the maid spoke, she let the cool water fall upon the head of Keo Fa. And as the Princess was enjoying its coolness, something hard and quite small dropped into her hair. She reached up to find out what it was, and she felt right away that it was a ring.

For some reason, the Princess did not cry out in her surprise. She kept the ring hidden inside her closed fingers until the girl had gone off with the empty jar.

Then only did the Princess spread her fingers wide. Lo, there in her hand lay the most beautiful ring she ever had seen. A splendid big ruby was set upon its golden circlet. As fiery red as a sunset it was, and a rosy light shone all about it.

"Go back to the brook, Girl," Keo Fa called to the maid. "If that Prince is still there, see what he is doing. Tell me each word he says to you."

The little maid ran off to do her lady's bidding. And Keo Fa looked again at the ruby ring.

"Surely this is a royal gem," she thought. "Surely this young man is the son of some great King. By the will of Heaven his ring has dropped from his finger into my water jar. It must be a sign that he is the one I shall marry."

Keo Fa was young. But she was quite old enough to have already found a husband. It was as people said. Her father, the King, had no wish to lose his dear daughter. Many fine Princes had come seeking her as a bride. But her father had set such impossible tasks for them that they had had to go home without her. This had not mattered to Keo Fa. No one of these Princes had been greatly to her liking.

When the maid came back from her errand, she said to the Princess, "That good young man was still there. He was looking and looking about in the grass. He had lost a fine ruby ring, which his dear mother had given him. A magic ring, it was, he said, with a fire ruby which gives off a bright rosy light."

"Truly he is a Prince. And this is a sign straight from Heaven. I already feel love for him. Heaven has sent him to be my bridegroom." So ran the thoughts of the Princess Keo Fa.

"Go once more to the brook, Girl," the Princess said then. "Say to the Prince—for surely he is a Prince—'Your ring will come back to you by the hand of Keo Fa.'"

Her message brought joy to Sotat. He had already decided

to ask the King for his daughter in marriage. So he lost no time now in making his way to the palace.

As for the King, he never had seen such a handsome young man. Almost he was ready to give up his dear daughter to him. Almost he decided to do without the difficult tasks that would prove the youth to be worthy. But then he remembered how dearly he loved Keo Fa and how much he would miss her.

"Before you can wed my daughter," he said to Sotat, "you must perform the tasks I will set for you."

His servants brought forth a great basket of rice, which they set down at the feet of Sotat.

"Thousands and thousands of grains of rice are here in this basket," the King said. "We shall throw them all to the winds. Some will drop on our fields. Some will fall on our gardens. Some will be blown off into the forest. It will be your task to gather them all up again. Their number is known to us. They shall be counted once again, tomorrow at midday. If one grain is missing, there will be no wedding for you and Keo Fa."

Poor Prince Sotat! He took the big basket. And he began to pick up the grains of rice. One by one, he found them. But it took a long time. And he soon saw he would never be able to gather them all before the next day.

Kneeling there in the palace garden, Sotat raised his arms to the sky. "Heavenly Teacher, give me your blessing! Buddha, send help," he prayed. "Is it good in thy eyes that I should marry this Princess? Then send to me the birds and the insects and all the small creatures that crawl on the earth. Bid them aid me in this task."

At once the air was filled with sounds that brought joy to Sotat's ears. There was the chirping of birds. There was the humming of insects. Hundreds of tiny feet were pattering over the earth. For the birds, the insects, and the small animals all loved this good Prince.

The King could not believe his eyes the next morning. For every single grain of rice was there, back in the basket.

"Well done, Prince!" cried the King. "Now comes a second test. This time the rice shall be thrown in the river. Every tiny white grain must be found again if you are to marry Keo Fa."

On the riverbank, Sotat again held his arms high. He stretched them out over the water. And he called for help from the fishes, the eels, and all the other living things in that stream. Once more he prayed for the blessing of Buddha on his impossible task.

Next morning the rice basket was full. But, alas, one grain was missing.

"That grain of rice must be found or you cannot marry Keo Fa." The King's voice was glad. He still could put off parting with his dear daughter.

On the riverbank, then, Sotat called out in a loud voice, "O ye fishes, ye eels, and all river creatures! A rice grain is missing. One of you must have dropped it. None could be so cruel as to steal it from me. Until it is found, I cannot wed the King's daughter."

Slowly, slowly one fish swam out of a hiding place.

"Here is the grain of rice. I took it for myself. Among so many, I thought, how can one grain be missed?" That fish did not look up.

"Thief! Thief!" cried out the fish, the eels, and the other river creatures. "How could you do such a thing to a Prince so loved by Buddha?"

Sotat took the grain from out of the fish's mouth. In doing

this, however, his long forefinger touched the nose of the fish. And at once it was turned down, as if in shame.

"Ask pardon from Buddha!" the Prince said to the fish-thief. "Go to his temple. Bow your head before his golden statue. And pray that he will forgive you as I do."

That is why, so the Cambodian tale-tellers said, these fish have bent noses. That is why, too, each year with the Big Rains, they swim back up the Mekong to find the temple of Buddha.

Perhaps you would like to know whether this good Prince at last married his Princess. It is part of the story.

Sotat put the missing grain of rice into the basket. There should have been nothing now that the King could do to put off the wedding. But the jealous father quickly thought up one more test to make.

"First I must be sure that you truly love Keo Fa," he said to Sotat. "Tomorrow we shall have a great feast here at the palace. But, before we eat, I shall gather together all the fair maidens of the court. The daughters of my ministers, the daughters of the nobles, even the young maids who serve us shall I call into the great hall.

"All of them shall be hidden behind a wide screen. And each one shall thrust the tip of a finger through a different hole in the screen. Your heart, my fine bridegroom, will tell you which one of the fingertips belongs to Keo Fa. Choose with great care. And if you choose rightly, the world shall be told you are to marry my daughter."

Prince Sotat stood still before the wide screen. Carefully, carefully he looked at the long, long row of fingertips. Slowly

he moved along. Each fingertip seemed more slender and more finely pointed than the one before.

Suddenly he stopped. He had seen a rosy-red light, shining through the hole, around one of the fingers.

"It is the rosy-red fire from my dear mother's ring," he said to himself. And he remembered the words which the palace maid had spoken to him at the brook. "You shall have your ring back from the hand of Keo Fa." That was what she had said.

Quickly the Prince dropped down on one knee. Gently he laid his hand under the finger with the rosy glow. "This is my bride's finger," he cried. And so it was.

The two young people, the good Prince and his fair Princess, wept for joy. At their wedding there was feasting that lasted three days. There were the beating of gongs and the music of drums.

None of the songs on their wedding day was sweeter than those of the birds. By the thousands they flew into the Great Hall of the palace to sing for the good Sotat, who was as beloved on earth as he was in Buddha's Heaven.

Did fishes come to the wedding? That I cannot say. But if any were there, I am sure none among them had noses that were turned down. The "bent-nosed ones" would have been too ashamed to appear with that ugly reminder of their brother's wrongdoing.

THE SHAH WEAVES A RUG

In other times, the King of Persia was known as a Shah. As with the rulers of other countries, some Shahs were good. Others were not so good. But the Shah in this story was just about the best ruler Persia ever had had. Or that is what his people said.

Good people of that land, who obeyed its laws, truly loved him.

"Our Shah cares for us as if we were his own children," they declared. "He visits us in our homes. He gives money to our poor to buy food and clothes for their children. He sends his own doctor to heal us when we are sick. And he rewards our good deeds."

Bad people who did not obey the laws of their land were afraid of this Shah. For bad deeds, too, were rewarded. The arms of the prison guards were strong. The beatings they gave to wrongdoers made their backs sore for many days.

One might think it impossible for a great ruler like this Shah to find out which of his people were good and which were bad. But this one was clever, and his heart was big. Often he would hide his royal person beneath the rags of a beggar. Or he would put on the rough dress of a country farmer. No one knew who he was when he slipped out of his palace to walk on the city streets and along the country roads. Thus disguised, he could see for himself what was going on in the land.

There was a time when bad news was spread throughout the Shah's city.

"People are disappearing each night. No one knows what becomes of them." The word was brought to the ears of the Shah. "Ten are missing today. Twelve are gone from their homes and have not been seen for three nights." Day after day the same report was made. Wives came to the palace seeking their husbands. Also, husbands there were whose wives could not be found.

"I must look into this mystery for myself," the Shah decided. He straightway put on his rough farmer's dress. And he went out into the marketplace.

A great crowd was there that afternoon. People were selling and buying. And above the noise of many voices there rose sounds of sweet singing. The clear tones of the song rang on the air like the bells of a temple.

Under a spreading shade tree at one side of the busy square, men and women were gathered about a singer dressed as a Holy Man.

"What can this be?" The Shah stopped to listen at the edge of the crowd. "Who is this Holy Man? Why has he never been brought to sing for me at the palace?"

While the Shah wondered, the singer began to move backward. From under the shade tree, he backed, little by little, into a street that led out of the city. And all the while he was singing.

It was just as if his listeners were under a spell. For they moved, all of them, after him. Slowly, oh, slowly he led them on. Farther and farther they followed him, until the houses of that city were few and far between.

"This is indeed strange!" The Shah was more and more puzzled. And he went along to find out what it all meant.

At last the singer came to the walled courtyard of an ancient fort, which was no longer used. As if by some magic, its great gates were swung open. Still singing loud and clear, the man in the dress of a Holy One walked backward in through the gates. And his listeners, still spellbound, followed him.

"Truly these people are bewitched by this man!" The Shah shook his head. "I must see this to the end." And he, too, followed the singer in through the iron gates.

"Clang!" The great gates swung shut. With a thud, a huge iron bar dropped across them. Then it was too late.

The song died. A crowd of rough men, with fast-swinging clubs, rushed out of the fort and fell upon the dazed listeners. Soon every man and woman of them was tied, hand and foot, with strong leather straps. The Shah, in his farmer's dress, had no gentler treatment.

"What will you do with us?" the Shah asked of those who were dragging him into the fort.

"Sell you in the slave market in a neighboring land," his captors told him. "You are strong and well fed. You will bring a good price. Our caravan leaves here this very night. As soon as the moon shows its face over the rim of the desert, we will be on the way."

"So this is the answer to the mystery of those who have disappeared from their homes." It was all clear to the Shah now. Then he spoke aloud to his captors.

"But I will not bring you nearly as much money in the slave market as I could right here. There is a way in which I am worth very much more. Let me speak to your chief."

The men who had tied him up were about to refuse. But the leader of these bandits had heard his words. And he was always greedy for more money.

"Let the farmer speak," he commanded. "Let him tell us about this money he promises."

"A skilled weaver am I, O Chief, in spite of my farmer's dress." The Shad stood fearless before the wicked man, for the words he had spoken were true. When he was only a boy, he had learned from the palace weavers how to work at the looms. He loved the bright colors of the silk and wool threads. No one could weave a handsomer rug than could he.

"My fingers make magic on the weaving looms. The rug I can make for you will bring you three times my price as a slave." He may have seemed to be boasting. But he had to impress this chief.

"Go fetch a loom." The man's greedy eyes shone. "Let this weaver show us his magic. If he has not spoken truly, we can sell him in the slave market on our next journey."

Each day the bandits watched the Shah work at the loom. The chief licked his lips with delight when he saw the bright colors woven into a splendid pattern of flowers and birds.

"How many gold tomans* shall I ask for this rug?" he said when the Shah was near the end of its weaving.

---

* Persian coins.

"Five thousand gold tomans at least, O Chief."

"Five thousand tomans! Who would pay such a great sum?"

"The Shah himself would pay it, but I am told he is away from the city just now. Take it to his Queen. She also loves beautiful rugs. She will no doubt pay you that sum."

"You speak well, Weaver." The head bandit nodded. "I will take the rug to the Queen when you have finished its border."

The Shah's fingers flew faster now than ever before. Yet he seemed to be taking extra pains with the pattern on the rug's end. Flowers and birds to match its center could be seen along it. But also there were letters like those in the old Persian writings. The bandits had never seen letters like these before. Such writing was known only to those of royal birth in ancient times.

At last the Shah's rug was finished. The last letter was woven in. The last knot was tied in the fringe.

"I myself will go with the porter to carry the rug to the palace," the bandit chief cried. "With my own hands I will give it to the Queen. And if you are right, Weaver, I will come back here with five thousand gold tomans."

"You must not let the gatekeeper stop you," the Shah replied. "Nor the doorkeeper of the Queen's rooms. Unroll the rug only under the eyes of the Queen herself." The royal prisoner spoke earnestly. And he had a reason, as the tale will soon show.

"The Shah is not here. The Queen grieves for his absence. She will see no one." At first the guards would not let the bandit and his porter come into the courtyard.

"But I have a rich gift for the Queen." The bandit would not go away. "She will be angry if you do not let us come in."

So the gatekeeper let them pass. And they made their way

to the Queen's part of the Shah's mansion. There, too, the guard stopped them.

"I will take your gift to the Queen. And I will let you know if it pleases her." The doorkeeper there was about to turn the strangers away when the voice of the Queen came from behind the heavy curtains of silk.

"Let the stranger come in," she cried. "I will look at his gift. It will take from my heart a little of the worry I feel in the absence of my dear husband."

So the curtains were put aside. The bandit chief bowed low before the fine lady. And her dark eyes peered curiously over the veil which hid the lower part of her face.

When the rug was spread out, a cry of delight came from her lips. This was a rug of rare beauty, and much like those already highly prized in the palace.

Then the Queen gave another cry—a cry of surprise. She bent down to examine the end of the rug. So long did she look at it that it was as if she were reading a book. Then she spoke aloud.

"This is a rich gift, O Stranger," she said. "I accept it with pleasure. And what is its price?"

"Five thousand tomans for you, Royal Lady." The bandit bowed very low. "For another it would be more than twice that sum."

"Ten thousand tomans I will give, then. The rug pleases me well." Then, calling one of her guards, she added, "I myself will go with this man to count out the tomans. You, Stranger, shall wait here until we come back."

So it was that the Queen had a chance to give secret orders to the palace guards.

"Into the pattern of that rug," she told them, "our Shah has woven a message for me. He calls for help. This very man who has brought me the rug holds him a prisoner in the old fort beyond the west city walls.

"When these men take their leave, follow them at a distance. Give orders to fifty of our best warriors to come after you. And make sure that the gates of the fort do not close before you can rescue the Shah."

The bandit chief, of course, knew nothing of the message which the Shah had woven into the rug's border. In his joy over his bags of gold he never turned round. He did not see the Shah's soldiers, who were following him.

It so happened that when the chief and the porter came back, the false Holy Man was singing his way once more in through the gates. Another group of bewitched listeners was following him as before.

The wicked chief stopped to let them pass inside the iron gates. His cruel eyes gleamed with satisfaction as he watched the last one go to his doom. Then he started to follow.

But before he could enter the courtyard, the fifty strong palace soldiers had fallen upon him. Before the gates could swing shut, they had captured its guards. They had seized the false Holy Man with the sweet singing voice, and they had tied up the bandit chief.

With their shining swords the Shah's men had no trouble in taking over the fort. Quickly they freed their beloved Shah, and also the newly arrived men and women who had fallen under the spell of the singer.

You can guess what happened then. When they came to their senses, these men and women fell on their knees before the good Shah, who had saved them from the slave market. With the other people of that great city, they rejoiced when the wicked chief and his band were put to death in the public square.

"Blessed be our Shah!" Shouts rang out. "Blessed be the loom on which he wove the rug that saved our lives! Blessed be all weavers whose patterns tell stories."

"Blessed be weavers!" This saying was heard all over that ancient land of Persia. And from that day to this, that country has been famous for its beautiful rugs.

THE PRINCESS IN THE CAMPHOR TREE

People of olden times thought more about spirits and fairies than we do today. Many were sure that such magic beings flew through the air, that they lived in the streams, that they had homes in the trees.

The fairies and spirits could help men. Or they could do them harm. Sometimes, it was said, a fairy would turn herself into a girl. She would come into the hut of a lucky young hunter to be his wife.

That is how it was in this old tale of the Princess who lived in a camphor tree in Malaya on the other side of the world.

Of all the camphor gatherers in that land, an old man named Bongsu was by far the cleverest. All his life long, Bongsu had collected the gum of the camphor trees in the jungle forests. Over his campfire he had boiled it down until it made crystals as white as a cloud in a summer sky.

Bongsu could spot a full camphor tree at first sight. Other hunters had to smell chips of its wood. Or they looked for bits of camphor gum in its bark. But this old camphor hunter would just lay his hand on a tree trunk and say, "Here is much camphor."

And it would be so. As soon as the tree's bark was cut, the forest would be filled with the sharp smell of the camphor. And Bongsu would have plenty of crystals to sell to those who used camphor for medicines, and for other things, too.

But, like all men, Bongsu grew old, very old. At last he was too old to go out with his seven sons to hunt camphor trees in the jungle. They had to set forth without him, with their carrying baskets on their backs, and their chopping knives in their hands.

Each time the seven brothers went forth, however, the parting words of their father rang in their ears.

"Take care, my sons. Do not anger the Bisans, those spirits who live in the camphor trees. Remember, if one of you tells a lie, the Bisans will know it. Let one of you take one grain of rice more than your share and they will blind your eyes so that you cannot find even one camphor tree. Work well. If you are lazy, if you take even a little time out to oil your hair, your carrying baskets will be empty.

"And above all," the old man always said, "do not forget to make the rice offering for the Bisans. Sing your prayer loudly that they may guide you to the full trees."

Usually the seven brothers all remembered the words of their father. But there was once a time when one did not. The six older brothers worked well. The seventh and youngest, whose name was Kepang, helped them at first. He swung his chopping knife well as they cut their way into the jungle. He gave a strong hand in the building of the wood hut for their shelter.

When it was time for the rice offering, young Kepang sang as loud as the others, inviting the Bisans to come to the rice feast.

> Bisans! O Bisans!
> Spirits of the camphor tree!
> Come, come eat the rice
> We have put here for thee.

That is how they called the camphor spirits to their hut, where the rice grains had been spread about.

> Bisans! O Bisans!
> Show us the way
> To the trees full of camphor.
> Lead us, we pray.

The first evening young Kepang sang this prayer along with his brothers. But when morning came he seemed to forget all about gathering camphor.

All day he spent on the banks of the river that cut through the jungles. Sometimes he fished. More often he slept under a tree. And there was no camphor at all in his basket when night came.

One day, two days, three days it was like that. It was as if the young man were under some spell. And his brothers were angry.

"You are lazy, Kepang," they cried. "The Bisans will be angry, and our father will scold."

"Perhaps I shall not go home with you to hear his angry words." This was all the young man would say. Oh, indeed it was just as if a Bisan had bewitched him. He was still lying asleep on the bank of the river at the end of seven days, when his brothers went home.

The tale does not explain why Kepang acted so strangely. But perhaps what happened next had something to do with it.

The young man was walking along the edge of a stream when he came to a clear pond under a waterfall. There, bathing herself in the white falling water, was a beautiful girl. Surely she was a Princess, Kepang thought, a Bisan Princess perhaps.

For she was as beautiful as the moon. Her eyes were bright as two stars. Her long dark hair fell to her ankles, covering her like a shining black cloak. It is no wonder that the young camphor hunter fell in love with her at first sight.

Softly, softly, Kepang crept toward her. The song of the waterfall smothered the sound of his footsteps. And the girl did not see him until he was at her side. Gently he caught hold of her long shining hair. And he drew her into his arms.

With a cry, the Bisan Princess turned to look into the face of the young camphor hunter. Kepang's dark eyes were soft. His smile was gentle and kind. The girl, too, felt love come into her heart.

"What do you want of me, young Stranger?" the Bisan Princess asked then.

"I want you for my wife," he answered tenderly. "I will love you well if you will come to live with me in my village."

Kepang took her hand in his. He started to lead her down the path that led out of the jungle.

"I could love you, too, Kepang." The Princess felt her heart melting. "I could be your wife. But a Bisan like me could not live in a village. Only in my camphor forest could I be truly happy."

So in love was Kepang that he allowed the Bisan girl to take him with her far into the jungle. The birds above them sang sweetly. The plants and the jungle vines seemed to swing apart to let them pass through.

At last they came to a tall camphor tree. Its green leaves shone brighter than those of any other tree in that forest. And in its thick branches, high up above the jungle floor, Kepang saw a little wood house.

"This shall be our home," the Princess told him. "Here we can be happy together."

And so they were, for a full seven days.

But at the end of that time the bride saw that her young husband no longer was smiling.

"Why are you sad, Kepang?" she asked. "Why do you not eat the good rice and the fresh fish in your eating bowl?"

"I long for my village, dear One," Kepang replied. "I think of my father. He is old. He must be missing me. I must pay him a visit to let him know all is well with me. Yet how can I go home with no camphor in my carrying basket?" Now at last the young man was sorry he had not worked along with his six brothers.

"Bring your basket to me," his bride said to Kepang. And when he set it down at her feet, she waved her slender hands over it. She sang a sweet magic song to the camphor tree. And a shower of white camphor crystals rained into the basket. She did not stop making her magic upon it until it was filled to the top.

"Go back to your father, dear Kepang. Tell him all is well with you. But say nothing else. Your brothers will ask where you found this pure camphor. But you must not tell them. Say no word of our marriage or you will not see me again. And promise me, promise me that after seven days you will come back to me."

Old Bongsu rejoiced when Kepang returned. The six older brothers looked with envy at his basket filled with white camphor. None they ever had made themselves was so pure as Kepang's. None brought such a high price in the marketplace.

Kepang could now pay all his bills. And at the end of seven days, to his brothers' surprise, he lifted his carrying basket onto his back. Then he went off by himself again into the camphor forest.

The Bisan Princess was joyful, and she made a fine feast to celebrate her husband's return. "Now we can be happy together here for ever and ever," she said.

But when seven more days had gone by, Kepang again grew unhappy.

"I miss my father and my brothers," he told his Bisan bride. "I miss my friends in our village. O my dear Wife, let us both go there and make it our home." He talked and he talked, he begged and he begged, until at last his fairy wife gave in.

"I will go to live in your village, Kepang," she consented. "But you must build me a little house where I can be quite alone and safe from curious eyes. Never must we tell anyone about our home here in the camphor tree. That must be a deep secret. So, too, must the magic camphor songs I have taught you.

"If the King of this land should ever hear the magic songs— if he ever should know that I am a Bisan who lived in a camphor tree—he will carry me away from our hut.

"Of course, I could escape from him," the fairy girl continued. "I could easily turn myself into a locust and fly out of his palace. But then I could never become a human again."

Kepang was careful. Out in the jungle, he sang the magic

songs only when the other hunters were far away. None knew
that it was the Bisans who showed him the full trees.

The young couple was happy. They loved each other truly.
And they doted upon the baby boy who, in time, was born
to them. The child was a fine little fellow indeed. He was as
strong as his father and as beautiful as his mother.

The camphor which Kepang brought back from his jungle
hunts was still finer than that of any other young man. He
soon became rich, and the story of his good fortune came to
the ears of the King.

"I am called to the palace," Kepang told his dear wife one
day. "And I am afraid. What shall I do if the King asks for
the secret of my pure camphor?"

"Answer his questions, my Husband. If he asks the secret of
your camphor, just tell him you can smell a good tree farther
than other hunters. Tell him you have lucky dreams that show
you where pure camphor can be found. But do not sing for
him any of my magic songs."

It was the magic songs, however, which that King wanted
to hear. News of the young hunter's singing somehow had
come to him.

"Sing me the camphor songs or you shall die," the King
said to Kepang. His voice was hard. He meant what he said.

So Kepang was forced to sing the words his Bisan Princess
had taught him. They must have floated out of the palace over
the air to his own hut. And his dear wife must have heard
them. For Kepang had no sooner finished one of the songs
than a brown locust flew in through the window of the King's
palace. It buzzed round his head, and somehow he knew it was
his fairy wife, who had turned herself into the insect.

"Alas, my dear Husband." Now it was her human voice

which he heard. "It is as I warned you. You have sung the secret song. Never again can I be human again. I must go back to the camphor tree." Then she flew out of the window.

Somehow or other, Kepang escaped from the palace guards. Somehow he managed to follow the buzz of the locust back to their hut, where their small son was playing in the dooryard.

Kepang quickly stood the child upright inside his carrying basket. With this slung on his back, he ran off to follow his locust-wife along the jungle path.

All would have been well had Kepang not stumbled over a tree root. The child was thrown out of the basket onto the jungle path. And, as he fell, his head struck the point of the chopping knife in his father's belt. Luckily, the little boy was not badly hurt. There was only a deep cut over one eye.

Kepang was running so fast to keep up with the locust that he did not notice the child's fall. Other camphor hunters later found the boy and dressed the wound over his eye. They took him to the home of old Bongsu, his grandfather, who cared for him tenderly until he was grown.

As time went by, the village people put together the story of Kepang and his Bisan bride. They told it whenever they saw the boy with the scar over one eye. And if a camphor hunter dreamed of this child, he knew he would not have any luck in the forest the next day. As for Kepang and the Bisan Princess who lived in the camphor tree, they never were seen again.

THE WOULD-BE WIZARD

In Arabia, long, long ago, there once lived a stupid man who did not like to work. Kassim was his name, and he was well known in his part of the city of the Great Caliph.

"You are as lazy as Kassim," fathers used to say to their sons when they were slow to bring water home from the well. Of boys who would not learn to read and write, they would ask, "Do you want to grow up with no more wits than Kassim?"

Everyone pitied poor Kassim. They were even more sorry for Kassim's wife, who was so much brighter than he. But there came a time when their pity was no longer needed. Strange to tell, Kassim suddenly became rich and a favorite of the Great Caliph.

Part of it was luck. Part was that Kassim's wife was so wise. And part came from the woman's strange name, "Jarada," which in ancient Arabic meant "Locust."

Try as she would, Jarada could not make her husband do any kind of hard work. This job and that job she found for him. But he would only yawn and say, "Oh, that would be far too hard for me."

"There is no food in our house, Kassim," Jarada, at last, said to her lazy husband. "You must find some way to earn money or we shall starve."

"Who would pay Kassim money for anything he could do?" Her husband actually laughed. He did not seem at all ashamed of his bad fame. And then he added, "I would indeed be a wizard if I were to earn money."

At the word "wizard," however, Jarada wrinkled her brow. An idea had come to her.

"Why should you not become a wizard?" she asked Kassim. "Those makers of magic do nothing but sit under a tree in the marketplace. They are paid well for their charms that bring good luck and for the words they speak to those who come to them for advice."

"But how can I make charms, Jarada?" I do not know how to write. All letters of the alphabet are the same to me."

"Stupid one, it is not with letters that magic charms are made," his wife replied. "A wizard only makes marks. He makes many marks upon paper. Straight marks and curly marks. That's all you need do. No one has ever understood the writing of a lucky charm."

"But to give people advice? How could a stupid man like me give advice?"

"Oh, just say to them whatever comes into your mind. Tell them you have talked with the stars, and they will believe whatever they like."

Well, being a wizard did not sound very hard, the lazy man thought. So he opened the long pen case which his wife brought home from the market the next day. He dipped the end of its reed pen into the wee inkpot in its end. And he began to make marks on a small sheet of paper. With the tiny spoon from the case he sprinkled fine sand to dry up the ink. His wife cried out in delight that he had made a fine charm.

Taking his seat under a tree in the marketplace, Kassim began to cry out, "Allah has made me a wizard. Now I can read the stars. I write good-luck charms. Come to me with your troubles."

Those who knew Kassim laughed until their sides ached. But others were strangers from neighborhoods far away. They did not know how very stupid this would-be wizard was. Some of these that very first day thought they needed a good-luck charm. How else should they turn away the Evil Eye of the spirits which might be hovering near them?

A charm against the Evil Eye! A paper to keep sickness away! A secret spell against a bad neighbor! All these and more charms did Kassim pretend to make. And he sold them for much money. Being a wizard was no trouble at all. Jarada, his Locust, could now buy all the food she could wish for. She soon had enough also to pay for a new, red silk head shawl.

All went well with the would-be wizard until one day a woman from the palace of the Great Caliph came to ask him for help.

"O Wise Wizard, I am in trouble," she said. "I have a secret which none other must know, and I do not see clearly how I shall act."

"Your secret is safe with me, Woman. No one shall hear it from me," Kassim assured her.

"Well, I am a thief, but indeed I did not mean to steal." The woman began to cry. "I am the handmaid of the wife of our

Great Caliph. And one day in the palace I found his fine golden ring, which he left on the rim of the bathing pool.

"The Evil One himself must have guided my fingers. For I picked up the ring and hid it under my dress. Now the Caliph has missed his ring. He has said he would punish the thief who has taken it. Ask the stars, O Wise Wizard, whether the Caliph will learn of my wrongdoing."

It was not yet night, but the first stars could be seen. Kassim turned his eyes upward toward their twinkling lights. He opened a little black book, from which he pretended to read magic words.

"You are truly in trouble, Woman," he warned. "You must get rid of the ring quickly. Drop it into the water jar which stands at the door of the Caliph's great hall, or you will be found out and put to death." Sometimes this Kassim was not nearly so stupid as people thought.

The frightened woman trembled at the wizard's words. "Better lose the ring than my head," she cried. She put a gold coin into Kassim's outstretched hand. Then she hurried away.

When she heard the story, Kassim's wife went at once to her friend who was cook for the Great Caliph.

"My husband talks with the stars," she told her friend. "He knows many secrets. He could, I am sure, find the Great Caliph's ring."

So Kassim was called to come to the palace. There also he raised his eyes to the sky to consult the stars. He opened his little black book of magic. He made many, many black marks on a piece of paper, which no one could understand.

Then he led the way to the water jar that stood by the door of the great hall. "The stars tell me your ring is here, Sire," he said to the Caliph.

Of course the ring was there. And of course this false wizard went away happy, with a purse full of gold.

Kassim was not left in peace very long. Soon thereafter another robbery took place at the palace. This time it was a chest full of jewels and gold pieces that disappeared.

"Find my chest for me, just as you found my ring," the Caliph commanded when Kassim stood before him. "Speak to the stars. Look in your black book of magic. And write what you please in your charms. But bring me back quickly my gold and my jewels."

Now Kassim had no idea at all where the treasure chest was. To gain time, he said, "This task is more difficult, O Caliph. I shall need forty days to uncover its hiding place." Surely, he thought, in forty days Heaven would send him help.

"Forty days, then, but no more," the Caliph agreed. "If at the end of forty days you do not find my chest, you shall be left in the desert to die."

"It shall be as you say, Great One." The unhappy Kassim bowed low. Then he hurried away home to tell his wife of his trouble.

It happened that the Caliph's treasure chest had been stolen by a robber band. Forty of these thieves there were, just the same number as the days Kassim had to discover where it was hidden.

These robbers were not long in learning that the Caliph had called on Kassim the Wizard to find the treasure.

"The man found the hiding place of the gold ring," the robber chief said to his band. "It may be indeed that he speaks with the stars. It may be he will find out that it is we who have stolen the treasure. Let one of us go and listen at Kassim's window, to see what he knows."

Their spy came while poor Kassim was telling his wife that he had no more than forty days in which to find the chest.

"O Jarada, my wife," the thief heard him say, "one of those forty is passing."

The spy waited to hear no more. He thought that by "forty" the man meant his own robber band. He ran off to tell the others that the wizard had known he was at the window, without even seeing him.

"'One of those forty is passing.' Kassim spoke these very words. How could he already know it was we who took the treasure?"

Greatly alarmed, the thieves sent another spy the very next evening. This one, too, could hear through the window what Kassim said to his wife.

"Jarada, my wife," he heard, "one of the forty has come and gone. Now a second is passing." Kassim was talking about the forty days, of course. But this spy, too, was sure he had in his mind the forty thieves.

"Kassim knows all," the chief said when the second spy had told what he had heard. "We must go and ask for his mercy. We may perhaps buy his silence with part of the treasure."

It truly may be that Kassim was not quite so stupid as people used to think. Or it may be that his wife told him what to say. For when the robber chief begged for his silence, this is the answer he gave:

"I will not tell the Great Caliph who the thieves are," he agreed, "but he must have his treasure back. Every jewel and every golden coin must be in the chest when I lead the Caliph to its hiding place. If not, I shall say that you forty were the thieves."

"Better give up the treasure than lose our heads." The robber chief shrugged his shoulders. And he showed Kassim the dusty bush on the edge of the desert beneath which they had buried the chest.

This time the Great Caliph was so pleased with Kassim's magic that he built him a fine house not far from his own palace. He gave the would-be wizard many bags of gold. And each time visitors came to his palace, he called on Kassim to show off his remarkable powers.

"Kassim talks with the stars," the Caliph boasted one day. "He can tell what is going on behind a thick curtain or wall. He does not need to see for himself.

"Here, I will show you. Kassim shall say what I hold inside my fist." The Caliph held out his right hand with his fingers curled tight.

Of course, Kassim, poor fellow, had no idea what there might be inside the fist of the Caliph.

Whenever he was in trouble, this false wizard always longed for his wise wife. Now he thought about her. He wished she were near to tell him what to do.

Should he say the wrong thing, his Caliph would be put to shame before his guests. He, Kassim, could lose his fine house. He could even be sent out to the desert to die of thirst. Forgetting where he was, he cried out, "Jarada! Jarada! Caught at last!" Which was to say, "Locust! Locust! Caught at last!"

Shouts came from the guests. For the Great Caliph had opened his fist at Kassim's words—and a brown locust had flown out before their very eyes.

"O Jarada," the lucky man said that evening, "Allah* saved

---

* Allah is an Arabic name for God.

me once more. But such luck cannot last. I must tell the Caliph
the truth. I must let him know, once for all, that I am no
wizard, that I do not really make magic."

"Then surely he will send you out to die in the desert. No,
we must find some other way." The man's wife was thinking
hard.

"I have it," she cried. "You shall tell the Caliph that Allah
has sent a sickness upon you. You shall say that this sickness
has taken away your wizard's power, so that you can no longer
make magic. Then never will he put you to the test again."

At first the Caliph would not believe the message which
Kassim sent him. He called him to the palace so that he could
see for himself whether the man was sick The former wizard
acted well the part of a madman. He tore his hair and his
clothing. He moaned and he laughed. Then he sang songs
without any words.

Kassim even pretended he did not know the Great Caliph.
At one point he grabbed the mighty ruler roughly by the arm
and pulled him out through the door of the great hall. Those
in the company followed, all greatly afraid.

But, for a third time, good luck saved Kassim. Hardly had
they left the hall when the roof tumbled in. With a roar and a
crash, its falling wood covered the place where the Caliph
had been standing a few moments before.

"Allah works through this man!" Wonder was written on the
face of the Caliph as he continued. "Without his wits, Kassim
is wiser than any one of us. Today he has saved our lives. He
shall henceforth live in peace in the house I have given him.
Our doctors shall calm him. And no one shall ever ask him to
make magic again."

THE BIRD THAT TOLD TALES

Once, when the world was new, other birds besides the parrot and the myna bird could talk with the words of men. And of all these others the one which could speak the most clearly was the sao in the jungles of Thailand.

In those ancient times talking birds were more clever than those of later days. At least they did more than merely echo the words which were spoken in their hearing. They could think for themselves. They could tell their thoughts as clearly as you or I can. Those who first told this story declared this was so. And this story itself gives the reason why they no longer do.

One day a certain farmer in Thailand, a man called Balat, caught a sao bird. It had lit on a tree on the edge of his rice fields. With a net on a long pole, Balat easily brought it down.

The tale does not say how big a sao was. Nor what colors there were in its feathers. It tells only that Balat tamed the bird well. It would sit on his shoulder. It talked to him just as if it were one of his children.

This bird had sharp eyes. From its perch by the door of Balat's house it saw everything that went on. The farmer's children and his servants took care to do what was right. For they knew, if they did not, the bird would tell its master.

For a time Balat enjoyed this talking bird. He liked to hear the tales it told him each evening. He was pleased that his sao was so wise and so clever.

But there came a time when the bird told a tale upon its own master. It was a tale of wrongdoing. And that did not please Farmer Balat at all.

On that day, Balat's next-door neighbor, a good man named Chai, was away from home. He was spending the day at the market in the nearby town. While he was gone, Balat stole his young water buffalo. The sao bird, of course, saw him bring the beast into their farmyard. With its bright beady eyes, the bird watched his master kill the animal.

"Oh! Oh!" the sao called out to the other birds in the nearby trees. "My master has killed Chai's water buffalo. He is eating some of its meat. Now he is hiding the rest in his own rice house." And the other birds chirped and squawked while they, too, looked on at these wicked deeds.

"Ai! Ai!" Chai wailed when he came home and found his buffalo gone. "Who will pull my plow for me now? Who will help me to turn over the earth in my rice fields?" His water

buffalo was the best helper this farmer had. No wonder he was sad. No wonder he went hither and yon, searching for the lost beast.

"Have you seen my buffalo, Friend Balat?" he asked of his neighbor.

But that wicked man only shook his head.

"How should I have seen your buffalo, Chai? I have been weeding my rice field all this day long." Balat did not mind at all telling a lie.

Chai was turning away to go on with his search when there was a fluttering of wings on the wooden perch by Balat's door. Loud and clear came these words from the excited sao bird there.

"Oh! Oh! Balat tells a lie. He did not weed the rice field all day. He killed Chai's young buffalo. Ate part. Hid part in his own rice house."

Before the bird's angry master could stop him, Chai had opened the door of the rice house. There between the rice bags, true enough, he found the buffalo meat which his neighbor had hidden.

"It was not I," Balat cried, aiming a blow at the head of the tale-telling bird. "Someone else must have put the meat in my rice house when I was away in the fields. This sao tells lies." He aimed another blow, but the bird darted to the other end of the perch. There it spoke up again.

"Indeed, it was Balat. I saw him. Killed buffalo. Ate part. Hid part in his rice house." Shrill and clear the words came.

"We shall take this to the judge," Chai cried out then. And he ran off to find the headman of the town, who decided such quarrels between neighbors like these.

Balat would gladly have wrung the neck of his sao. But he was afraid.

"The bird is a witness. If I do not let it come before the judge, it will be known that the bird told the truth. It will prove I was afraid to let it speak. I must find a way to make it seem that the bird is telling a lie."

The time for the trial was set for the next morning. And that night strange things took place on the farm of this wicked farmer, Balat.

Before the moon had opened its eye in the night sky, the farmer lifted the sao bird off its perch. He set it down inside a huge empty water jar, on which he put a tight cover made of black silk. Enough air came through it so that the bird could breathe, but it could not get out.

The night was clear. The moon shone bright. But the poor sao could not see even a glint of its light inside the dark, covered jar.

As the bird crouched on the bottom of the clay jar, it heard a pitter-patter upon its tightly drawn cover. It was a sound like that of rain, for the farmer was sprinkling the black cloth, little by little. Then the drops of water came faster, faster and faster. Soon it was as if rain were falling in torrents.

At the same time, sly Balat was beating with a stick upon the side of the hollow jar. What a noise his blows made! They were like claps of thunder. And that is what the sao bird was sure they must be.

"It is strange there should be a storm at this time of year," the bird thought. "But I hear water falling. The voice of thunder is calling."

Well, that was a bad night which the sao spent shut up in the jar. But at last morning came. The sun shone. The time for the trial was at hand.

Balat lifted the sao bird out of the jar, and he carried it off

to the court of the judge. His neighbor, Chai, was there, too;
and the trial began.

"My neighbor, Balat, killed my buffalo, O Judge." Chai
told his story. "He says he did not, but his own sao bird saw
him. The bird itself told me how Balat ate part of my buffalo
and how he hid part in his rice house. And there, O Wise
Judge, I found buffalo meat."

From the shoulder of the thief, the sao once more told on
its master. "Balat killed the buffalo. Ate part. Hid part inside
his rice house."

The judge and the people who were gathered at the trial
were astonished. What a clever bird this was! Surely it must
have happened just as the sao said.

"Then Balat shall be put into prison! He shall pay Chai for
the buffalo and——"

Here the judge was interrupted by a cry from Balat. "Will
you put me in prison on the word of a lying bird?" he shouted
at the judge. "The bird does not see clearly. It does not know
what it is saying. Let us put the sao to the test. Ask it a
question to which we all know the answer. Ask this lying
bird just what kind of weather we had here last night."

This made the judge pause.

"Every man who comes to me shall be fairly treated," he
said. "We shall ask the bird the question which Balat suggests.
Tell us, Sao Bird, what kind of weather did we have here last
night?"

Now you shall see how smart was the trick of this wicked
farmer. The bird could only remember how dark it was in the
water jar. He could still hear the pitter-patter of water upon its
tight cover. And the noise like the thunder!

"It was a dark, stormy night, Judge," the bird began. "Rain

fell. Thunder roared. It was a strange night for this time of year. But that's how it was."

"The bird does tell lies," someone in the crowd cried. "Last night the moon was bright. No drop of rain fell. Truly this bird does not tell the truth."

Balat was pleased with the success of his trick. "O Wise Judge," he cried, "it is as I have said. The sao does not see clearly. It could not tell whether the one who killed Chai's buffalo was Balat or some stranger. There is no proof it was I."

Poor Chai! He was sure that the bird spoke the truth, but he could think of no way to convince the judge.

So Balat went free. On the way home, the man did his best to wring the bird's neck. "You would tell tales on your master, would you, you ungrateful bird!" he cried out.

"I spoke only the truth, Master." The bird did not know just what had happened. But of one thing it was sure. It did not pay to speak the truth among men. Men were too smart for birds.

"Your end is here, Sao. Never again shall you sit on your perch by my door and spy upon me." With these words the farmer tried to twist the bird's neck. But the sao slipped from his hands. With a flash of its wings, it was gone, far into the jungle. The farmer, Balat, never saw it again.

Safe in the deep woods, the sao called to the other birds. "Hear my tale, Friends," it began. "Hear what befell me when I told the truth among men."

As the sao spoke, its eyes fell upon two strange bright birds from a neighboring land. "What birds are these?" it asked. And, to its surprise, they answered him with the words of men. They could speak as clearly as any sao.

"I am the parrot," said one, whose feathers were as bright as the sunrise.

"I am the myna," the other one cried. His shining black head had bits of bright gold upon it. "We can both of us speak with the words which men use."

"Then take care, O Strangers," the sao bird warned them. "Take care what words you speak out of your own minds, lest you come near to death, as has happened to me. With my own eyes I saw it happen, my master killing that buffalo. And I told only what I saw.

"But men are smarter than birds. My master made a fool of me. He tricked me into saying a fair night was stormy. He dropped water upon my jar cover so that it sounded like rain. He made a noise like the thunder. But I did not know these things then. For telling of how they seemed to me, I almost lost my life.

"Be warned, Parrot and Myna! Perhaps you will someday be caught and taken to live in the houses of men. It is good to have them give you shelter and food. But take care how you speak to them. Say only the words which your master puts into your beaks. Never, never speak thoughts that are not of his thinking. Only then will you be safe."

And that is why, so the old tale-tellers say, the parrot and the myna and all other talking birds never give us of their own wisdom. They know from the sao that it is better just to echo their masters' words.

THE UNLUCKY SHOES OF ALI ABOU

In Baghdad there once lived a rich man named Ali Abou. He had a fine house. And he had plenty of money.

Everyone in that Arabian city knew Ali Abou was rich. But no stranger would have guessed it from the old clothes he wore.

"Why should this Ali Abou not be rich?" his neighbors often asked one another. "He never spends a single dinar* on himself. Just look at his shoes." And then they would laugh.

Even the children of Baghdad used to laugh at the shoes of Ali Abou. They were so old. Some people said this rich man had worn the very same shoes all his life long.

How could shoes last so many years? Well, when there came a hole in them, Ali Abou would go down to the Street of the Shoemakers.

"Put a patch over this hole," he would say. Sometimes a shoemaker would shake his head and reply, "This shoe can no

* An Arabian gold coin.

longer be patched." Then Ali Abou would go to another, and another, until at last he would find one who would put on the patch. And it did not matter to him if the patch did not match the color of his shoes.

More holes, more patches! And more different colors! In his neighborhood, friends often said to each other, "May your luck last as long as the shoes of Ali Abou."

But there came a time when his old shoes brought bad luck to Ali Abou. It began one day when he was walking along the Street of the Glass Sellers.

"I have news for you, Friend Ali Abou," said one of the sellers of glass. "This day there has come here a man who has fine perfume bottles to sell. Flowers are painted upon them. You, who have money, should buy these beautiful bottles. Their price is not high—not more than sixty dinars. I can sell them again for you, a bit later on, for twice that sum."

Now Ali Abou was always trying to find ways to double his money. So he bought the fine painted bottles for sixty dinars.

From the Street of the Glass Sellers, Ali Abou walked along the Street of the Perfume Makers. And he came to the shop of a second friend, who had news for him.

"Ali Abou, there is in Baghdad this day a man selling rose water. Never has there been so sweet a perfume. The man will sell his rose water cheap, for only sixty dinars. And I can get for you twice that sum for it later on."

Here was another chance to double some money. So Ali Abou bought the rose water for sixty dinars.

At home Ali Abou poured the sweet rose water into his fine painted bottles. In a room at the back of his house, he set his treasures, high up, on a shelf under a window. There they would be safe, he thought, until the time came to sell them.

Well pleased with his morning was Ali Abou when he set out to visit the House of the Baths. It was his afternoon to go there to make himself clean.

He was just stepping inside when he met a friend, one Omar ben Adi, who was on his way out.

"Allah give you peace, Ali Abou," his friend greeted him.

"And to you also peace," replied Ali Abou.

Omar ben Adi's eyes fell on the feet of his rich friend. And he shook his head.

"O Ali Abou, you have much money. Why do you not buy yourself some new shoes? Those are the very worst shoes in all Baghdad. Truly, my Friend, you should have a pair of new shoes." And Omar ben Adi went away, still shaking his head.

When Ali Abou came out of the water, he dried himself well. He put on his long gown. Then he looked for his shoes.

But he did not find them. Somehow they had been pushed far, far back under a bench. Where his old shoes had been, there was now a pair of new shoes. Oh, they were fine new shoes, and just the same size as his own.

"My good friend, Omar ben Adi, has made me a present perhaps," Ali Abou thought as he looked at the handsome new shoes. "No doubt he bought them for me while I was in the bath. Indeed, these are far better than the shoes I was wearing." The man's heart was filled with thanks for his friend as he put on the new shoes and went off to his home.

But, as it happened, those new shoes were not a present from Omar ben Adi. They were the new shoes of the cadi, the judge of that part of the city of Baghdad.

The cadi, like Ali Abou, had come to wash himself clean at the House of the Baths. He had left his new shoes there by the bench when he undressed.

"Where are my shoes?" the cadi shouted as soon as he began to put on his clothes again. The bath men looked and looked. But they found only the patched old shoes of Ali Abou, far back under the bench.

They knew them at once. Who in all that city of Baghdad did not know those patched shoes?

"These are the shoes of Ali Abou," the cadi cried. "He has gone off with my new shoes. He has left these in their place. Who would have thought that rich man was a thief? Well, he shall be punished."

The cadi sent his servants to take the patched shoes to the house of Ali Abou. Of course, they found him wearing the fine new shoes of the cadi; and so they dragged him off to the angry judge.

"Ten blows on his back for Ali Abou, the thief! Throw him into jail. Do not let him come out again until he has paid a fine of one thousand dinars." These were the terrible words of the cadi.

Ali Abou tried to explain that it was all a mistake. But the cadi would not listen. Even if he had, do you think he would have believed such a silly story?

Well, Ali Abou paid the fine. And the first thing he did when he came out of the jail was to try to get rid of the shoes which had caused all his trouble.

"I'll throw them into the river," he said to himself. He smiled with pleasure at the splash his shoes made when they fell into the water.

But that same afternoon a fisherman's net brought the shoes out of the river again. And of course, by their patches, the man knew they belonged to Ali Abou.

"Perhaps that rich man will give me a dinar if I take his

precious shoes back to him," the lucky fisherman said to his wife.

It was too bad there was no one in the house of Ali Abou when the fisherman came. The doors were shut tight. Only one window was open, and that was high in the wall at the very back of the house. The man was tired with pulling his net up from the river.

"I'll not take the trouble to go away and come back again," he said to himself. "I'll just throw these shoes of Ali Abou's in through his window. He can pay me the dinar when I tell him I was the one who brought them back to him."

The shoes landed in the middle of the high shelf inside the window. They knocked down Ali Abou's beautiful painted bottles which had cost sixty dinars. Every one of them was broken. All their precious rose water was spilled.

"Woe! Woe!" Ali Abou wept when he came home that night. He beat his head against the wall, crying, "Those unlucky shoes! What bad luck they bring me. I must get rid of them at once."

It was dark when he took his shoes out into his garden. He scarcely could see. But he began to dig a hole to put them in, close to the garden wall.

The neighbors on the other side of the wall heard the noise of his digging. And out they came, running.

"Ho! We have caught you, Ali Abou," they shouted. "You are digging a hole under our wall. No doubt you are planning to creep through it and rob us. We shall take this to the cadi."

"So you are stealing again, Ali Abou!" The cadi did not give the unlucky man time to say even one word. "First you steal my shoes. Now you are planning to rob your neighbor. Back to jail you shall go! And you shall not come out again until you have paid a fine of one thousand dinars."

Again poor Ali Abou wanted to explain. Again the cadi would not listen. It would not have helped if he had. Who would believe a man would go out in the dark and dig a hole by a wall, just to get rid of a pair of old shoes?

Ali Abou wept when he paid the second fine of one thousand dinars.

"Somehow I must get rid of these shoes!" He could not get the idea out of his mind. Then he thought of a way. "I'll throw them into the sewer. The water will carry them off through the big pipe. No fisherman's net will pull them out of there."

But truly those shoes of Ali Abou were unlucky. For somehow or other, this time they stopped up the sewer. The dirty water ran out all over the street. This made a terrible smell, and the people complained. When the sewer was cleaned out, of course, there were the shoes of this same Ali Abou.

"He shall pay for cleaning the sewer!" The cadi's patience was nearing its end. "Twice as much as that costs shall he pay as a fine. And he shall stay in jail until every dinar is paid."

It took almost all the money of poor Ali Abou to set him free. His face was sad when he came home with his soggy shoes in his hand. Ali Abou washed the dirt from them. He made them as clean as he could. Then he set them on his doorstep to dry in the sun.

Now those unlucky shoes still smelled of the sewer. A strange dog, passing by, must have liked this strong smell. For it grabbed one of the shoes in its mouth and ran away with it. Ali Abou ran after the dog, but he could not catch it.

Why did that dog have to jump up on a garden fence? Why,

oh why did the heavy shoe have to slip out of the animal's mouth? But it did, and it fell on the head of a very small boy in the garden below.

The child cried and cried. In truth he was badly hurt. Many times did the doctor come before the child's head was well again.

What happened next? Well, of course, the child's father went to complain to the cadi.

"Ali Abou threw his shoe over my garden wall at my little boy. He all but killed the child. Who is to pay the doctor who saved my child's life?"

"Ali Abou shall pay." Now, indeed, the cadi was angry. This rich man with his old shoes made far too much trouble. "Ali Abou shall pay the doctor, of course. He shall pay twice the bill of the doctor as a fine. That will teach him to take care not to throw his old shoes over another man's wall."

Alas, this fine took every single dinar poor Ali Abou could borrow from his friends. He was now no longer Ali Abou the Rich but Ali Abou the Poor.

The cadi was surprised the next morning to see Ali Abou come of his own accord into the court. The man walked straight to the judge's table. He laid down upon it his pair of patched shoes. And before the judge could send him away, he shouted in a loud angry voice.

"This time it is I who come to complain, O Cadi. I complain of these shoes. I beg you to punish them for the things they have done to me. Put them in jail and never let them come out." He spoke as if his old shoes were live persons who could be blamed for their acts.

The cadi looked hard at Ali Abou. Was the man playing a joke? Or had he gone crazy? Well, he would let him speak on.

But Ali Abou was not joking. He was not joking at all.

"Yes, put these shoes in jail. Never let them come near me again. Write it down on a paper, Wise Cadi, that my shoes and I have nothing to do with each other."

The cadi could not help smiling now. Shoes were strange prisoners for his jail.

"These wicked shoes have caused all my troubles." Ali Abou was speaking again. "First they hid themselves under a bench in the House of the Baths. Thus I would think the cadi's new shoes were put into their place for me.

"Then they broke my fine painted bottles and spilled the rose water for which I had paid more than one hundred dinars. To put them out of sight, I tried to bury them by my garden wall, and my neighbors brought me before you.

"It was these evil shoes that stopped up the sewer. O Cadi, I was in no way to blame that a dog carried one off and dropped it on the head of the poor little boy.

"Four times, O Cadi, these shoes have sent me to jail. They have used up all my money. I want no more to do with them."

At last did the cadi hear the true story of poor Ali Abou and his unlucky shoes. He threw back his head and laughed. He laughed until the tears rolled down his cheeks. Each time he looked at the shoes he laughed again.

"Go in peace, Ali Abou," the cadi said kindly when he could stop laughing. "You have had enough trouble. Never again shall you see these wicked shoes."

This cadi, indeed, was not a hard man. Now he felt sorry for Ali Abou. He felt so very sorry that he gave him back all the dinars which the unlucky man had paid the court in fines.

What happened to the shoes? No one ever told that part of the story. But one thing is sure. They were never again seen on the feet of Ali Abou.

How the Dog Chose Its Master

Brahma is the name of the Great God of the Hindu peoples of Asia. It was Brahma, they say, who made the world and all the living things on it. And it was Brahma who sent the dog down from the heavens to choose its own master. At least that is the story which sometimes was told long, long ago.

The world had just been made. Its green land, its thick forests, its rushing rivers, and its deep oceans had all been put in their places. The time had come to make the creatures who should live in this world. It was time to make those whose homes should be on the land, the birds which should fly through the air, the fish which should swim in the sea.

"I will make man first," Brahma decided. "Then I will make woman, who shall be the wife of man.

"Now I will make the animals—the elephant and the tiger, the jackal and the rabbit." Brahma made so many wild animals that no one has ever been able to count them all.

He made other animals which could be tamed—the sheep and the cow, the horse and the goat, the water buffalo and the pig. And he set them all down upon the green land.

Last of all, while he was resting after so much work, Brahma made the dog. He was pleased with this animal, and he patted its head when he spoke to it.

It was not until much, much later that the followers of Brahma began to say that a dog was not a clean animal and to drive it outside their houses. In the beginning there was even a Hindu god known as the Heavenly Dog.

No, Brahma was truly pleased with the first dog. He taught it to wag its tail when he patted its head. He told it to bark when danger was near.

As to all his creatures, Brahma gave the dog work to do on the earth.

"You shall serve a master well, Dog," the Maker-of-All-Things commanded. "Where your master goes by day, there shall you go. Where he sleeps at night, there shall you sleep. But you shall rest always with one eye half open. Your ears shall listen for any strange sounds. You shall bark loudly to warn your good master of danger."

"Who shall my master be, Brahma?" the dog asked. As you may have heard, in those days, when the world was new, animals talked as well as gods or men.

"You shall find your master yourself, Dog. He will be the mightiest of all the living creatures on earth."

"But which creature is the mightiest, Heavenly One?" The dog was afraid he would not choose the right master.

"That you must find out for yourself," Brahma replied; and he set the first dog down on the land.

It was good to be on the green earth, so the dog thought. He ran and he jumped about. He drank at the brooks. He fed himself on the small animals, as Brahma meant him to do. And, all the while, he was looking and looking for the mighty creature whom he should serve.

"The mightiest would not be a bird in the air," the dog reasoned. "I myself am stronger and more powerful than most birds.

"My master could not be a fish in the sea. How could I follow a master who lives under the water? Surely the Great Brahma did not mean that a dog should live with a fish.

"No, it is clear that my master must be a land creature like me." The dog was trying hard to work out this puzzle for himself. "He must be the most powerful of all the living beings on the land. I will look for the creature who has no fear of any other. Him I will serve as Brahma has commanded." That is what the dog said to himself when he set out on his search.

The dog met many animals during his journey over the land. Some were smaller than he. They were afraid at the sight of him. Others were larger, like the sheep, the cows, and the pigs. But these also ran away from him when he growled and barked at them.

It was when the dog was walking along a forest path that he first saw the elephant. The huge beast was tearing branches off a tall tree. He was putting them into his mouth with his long trunk.

"Here is surely the largest animal on the earth," the dog thought as he backed away to a safe distance. "Surely this elephant is the strongest, since it can tear a tall tree apart. This must be the mighty master which Good Brahma means me to choose."

"Will you be my master?" the dog asked the elephant. "I will follow you by day. I will protect you by night. I will serve you well."

The elephant raised his long trunk into the air. He trumpeted his consent. And that night the dog slept close to the gray beast in the deep jungle. He has happy because he was sure he had found his own master.

The night was still young when there was a noise in the trees over their heads. A monkey was swinging from one branch to another. A twig broke with a loud snap, and the dog jumped up and barked. He barked as loud as he could, just as Brahma had taught him. It was his duty to warn his master that danger might be near.

Instead of being pleased, however, the elephant was angry.

"Stop barking, you silly dog." The great creature spoke softly. "You must not make so much noise in the night. The lion might hear you. In the dark, as well as by day, the lion hunts in the jungle, seeking its meat. If we are to be safe from him, we must keep quiet."

"Oho!" the dog thought. "This elephant is afraid of the lion. For all he is so big and so strong, he is not so mighty as this other beast. It is the lion who shall be my master."

So, when morning came, the dog said good-bye to the elephant. "You are not the mighty master whom the God Brahma meant me to choose." He excused himself as he went away, to go on with his search.

The dog hunted through the deep forest. He ran over the grassy plains. Of each animal he met, he asked the same question: "Do you, too, fear the lion?" And each one replied quickly, "Oh, every animal fears the lion. He is the king of all beasts."

"Have you seen the lion this morning?" the dog would ask then. And each animal replied, "No, I have not seen the lion. If I had, I would have run away and hidden myself."

So the dog was sure he had only to find the lion and tell him Brahma had sent him to serve him as his master.

On the edge of a small stream, the dog at last came upon the lion, drinking at a clear pool. Before the tawny beast could lift his shaggy head from the cool water, the dog began to speak.

"Brahma has made me, O Lion, to be the servant of the mightiest creature on earth. Surely you are that one. All the animals fear you—even the elephant. I will serve you well. I will hunt with you by day. By night I will warn you of danger. I pray, Lion, be my master."

Now the lion was a proud beast. The words the dog spoke pleased him. So he took him as his servant.

When darkness covered the jungle, the lion and the dog went forth to hunt. Suddenly a wind blew through the trees. The leaves rustled. And the dog, hearing these strange noises, began to bark.

"Hush, Dog! Be still!" The lion was snarling. "Never bark in the night. For man might hear you. Like a lion, man hunts when it is dark as well as when it is light. Bark and you will tell man where we are. Then he will kill me."

"Oho!" The dog's heart sank. "The lion fears man. For all his fierce snarling and his long teeth, the lion is not the mightiest creature on earth. He is not the master I seek."

"I see more clearly now." The dog was thinking hard. "Greatness is not just being big. It is not just being strong or fierce.

Man does not have tusks like an elephant. His teeth are not nearly so sharp as a lion's. Yet he is feared by the lion. At last I know surely whom Brahma meant me to serve."

So the dog went off to seek man, whom Brahma had set to rule over all living creatures. And in a clearing in the deep forest he came on the hut of a hunter.

"Take me for your servant, O Man." The dog stood before the hunter, wagging his tail. "Let me hunt with you by day. Let me warn you of danger by night. I will serve you well."

That night the dog slept at the door of that hunter's hut. When the wind blew through the trees, when a monkey threw a nut down on the ground, like a good watchman the dog barked.

"Good dog!" The hunter waked up to praise him. Then he went back to sleep. He knew he would be safe with his dog on guard at the door of his hut. As for the dog, he was happy. He knew that at last he had found the mightiest creature on earth.

ONE MEAN TRICK DESERVES ANOTHER

In a small village in Afghanistan there once was a man called
Assad who had a stupid son. They were quite different, Assad
and his son. For the father was clever. So clever was he that
every one spoke of him as Assad the Wise. The son was so
stupid that he was known as the Fool.

Almost anyone could trick this slow-thinking boy. And many
did. But it was a certain family of six brothers who played the
meanest trick on him.

One day Assad called the Fool to him. "You are to take our
nanny goat to the market," he said to the simple youth. "It
will not be too hard for you. She is a fine young nanny goat.
She will bring a good price. Drive her straight to the town.
Then come directly home with the money."

The Fool was delighted to have such an important errand to
do, all by himself. He sang as he set forth for the town, driving
the nanny goat in front of him. He took care not to let her go
off the road. He did not let her stop to nibble at the green

bushes along the way. No, he went straight toward the town, as his father had told him to.

They had safely covered a mile when the Fool met up with one of this family of six brothers. Somehow or other the six had learned of his errand. Secretly they had already planned to get his nanny goat for themselves.

"Good day, Fool," the first trickster saluted him. "Where are you taking that sickly old dog?"

The simple youth's mouth fell open in his surprise. "Why, this is no dog," he cried. "This is our young nanny goat. I am taking her to the market. I shall sell her for a good price, for, although she is young, she already gives milk."

The trickster laughed. He looked down at the goat. Then he looked at the boy. He shook his head sadly, as if that Fool was out of his mind. And he went away.

Around the next turn in the road, another of the six was waiting to greet the simple Fool. This was all part of their plan to get the nanny goat for themselves.

"Good day, Friend," said the second brother. "Where are you taking that sickly old dog?"

The Fool bent down to look closely at his young nanny goat.

"This is no dog, sir." He was puzzled now, and his voice was less sure. "This is our young nanny goat, who already gives milk. Truly she is no dog."

But the trickster only laughed.

"A nanny goat? Ho! Ho! This Fool does not know the difference between a nanny goat and a dog. Anyone with eyes in his head can see you are driving a sickly old dog." He too shook his head pityingly as he went on his way.

A third time, a fourth time, and a fifth time a different one of the brothers went through the same act. And when the sixth

had declared that the nanny goat was only a worthless old dog, the poor puzzled Fool said to himself, "My eyes must tell me lies. I must have left our nanny at home and taken this dog in her place. I'll just leave this dog here and go home for our goat."

This was just what the six brothers were waiting for. As soon as the boy was out of sight, they killed Assad's young nanny and made a feast for themselves.

"But, of course, you had the nanny goat," Assad told his son when he heard the story. "Those six brothers tricked you. But I know who they are. And I will get even with them for this trick."

The next day Assad himself took his old donkey out of the meadow behind his house. He put on its back a saddle with trimmings of silver. Its bridle of red leather was fit for the riding horse of a king.

On the back of this donkey Assad rode proudly along the road toward the house where the six tricksters lived. And, as he had hoped, he met one of them before he had gone very far.

"Good day," this one greeted him. "Pray, why do you put such a fine bridle and saddle on such a old donkey?"

"This is no donkey," Assad replied. "This is a 'bouchaki.'"

"A bouchaki? Whatever is a bouchaki?"

"Oh, a bouchaki is a magic beast." Assad did not smile at all. "A bouchaki is an animal which lives for one hundred years. And every night it spits out, at the feet of its master, a lump of pure gold."

The trickster ran home at once to tell his five brothers about this wonderful beast. They came out on the road, one by one, to have a look at it. And to each one Assad repeated the same impossible tale.

He had timed his ride well. He was just passing the house of the brothers when the sixth one appeared in the dusk.

"Truly, Friend, my bouchaki is a magic beast," he said. "If you will give us both shelter for the night, I will show you how it rewards me for its fine bridle and saddle."

The six watched Assad stoop down at the feet of his donkey. They saw him put his hand in the straw on their stable floor. And when he opened his fist, there, before their eyes, was a lump of shining yellow gold. None of the six noticed that he had taken the gold out of his own pocket before he bent down.

As soon as Assad and his bouchaki went away the next morning, the six brothers put their heads together.

"We must have for our own this magic beast that spits gold," they all agreed. "It would be cheap at a price of five hundred rupees."* And that is the fat sum which they offered Assad for his old donkey. Only they called it a "bouchaki."

Assad laughed until he cried when they led the donkey away. Then he said to his wife, "Those six who stole our nanny from our Fool will be angry tonight. They will find no lump of gold in the straw at their feet. Tomorrow they will come back here for their five hundred rupees. But I have another trick ready.

"You must tell them I have gone fishing." He explained what he meant to do. "Then you must say you will send for me. Set free one of our gray rabbits in the direction of the river. I will take its twin along with me. And you will see what will happen."

Assad's new trick worked well. The six brothers came early, but the donkey's former owner had already left home. None of

_____
* A rupee is a silver coin.

them saw him go. They did not know he had taken one of the twin rabbits off under his arm.

"My husband has gone fishing." Assad's wife spoke her piece well. "He is by now on the riverbank. But I'll send this rabbit to tell him you are here."

The six brothers were amazed to see the woman put the gray rabbit down on the ground. They could hardly believe their ears when they heard her say, "Run fast, good Rabbit! Tell my husband he is wanted back here at home." Wondering, they watched the rabbit bound away in the direction of the river.

All this time, Assad had been watching from a hiding place in a clump of bushes not far away. In a short time he came into sight of the six. Under his arm he was carrying the gray rabbit which he had taken away with him.

"Did that rabbit really give you our message?" one of the six brothers cried.

"Why else should I leave my fishing rod on the riverbank and come home?" Assad asked in return.

The amazed brothers whispered together. Forgotten was the bouchaki which did not spit gold. Once more they paid Assad five hundred rupees for a magic beast.

"They will come back, Wife," Assad declared. "They will be angry that they paid so much for an ordinary gray rabbit. And they will be ready to fight. Six against one is too many. I must make still one more plan."

He thought for a time in silence. Then he cried out, "I have it. I will kill our old billy goat, the one we are planning to eat. I'll smear your throat with its blood. Then I'll pretend I have killed you. When I bring you back to life again with my green rod, those brothers will think I have made magic once more." He told his wife just how she must act and what she must say.

"Give us our thousand rupees, Assad." The six brothers truly were angry when they returned. They had clubs and knives in their hands.

"Your bouchaki does not spit gold. Your rabbit does not carry messages. Give us our money back or we'll take your life."

"Very well," Assad replied. "Give me my bouchaki and my gray rabbit and you shall have your rupees." He knew very well that the rabbit would have run away when they tried to send it with a message.

"But before you go to get the animals, let us smoke a pipe of friendship together. Let us pretend I have forgiven you for tricking the Fool out of our nanny goat."

"Wife," he called to the woman, who could be heard moving about behind the curtains that shut off the woman's part of the house. "Wife, bring me my pipe. I will smoke with our guests."

When she did not appear, he pretended to be angry.

"Daughter of the Evil One!" he screamed. "Granddaughter of Demons, bring me my pipe now. You will be sorry if I have to come for it myself."

Assad played his part well. He rushed into the next room and pulled the curtains together after him. The amazed visitors heard the sounds of blows. There were screams from the woman. Indeed, she was quite as good at acting as her husband.

Then the man burst through the curtains, waving a bloody knife and dragging his wife behind him. Her neck and her shoulders were red with the goat's blood. She was moaning and groaning. Then she dropped to the floor, as if she were dead.

"That is your punishment for not obeying your master," Assad cried, looking down at her.

The watching six were struck dumb by the terrible sight. With wondering eyes they saw Assad next pick up a green rod from the corner of the room. Suddenly his anger seemed to be gone. He now gazed at his wife with a gentle smile on his face.

"Most of the time this woman obeys me at once," he said to his visitors. "Once more I have been too hard upon her. I will bring her back to life, just as I did the last time I killed her."

He drew the green rod back and forth slowly across the woman's bloody throat. Suddenly she opened her eyes. She rose to her feet. As if by magic she was as well and strong as before.

"Oh!" cried the six brothers. "Ah!" They looked at each other. This was the greatest wonder of all. Without saying a word, they knew they would give another five hundred rupees for this magic rod.

"We will forget the bouchaki and the rabbit if you will sell us this stick which brings the dead back to life," they told Assad.

And five hundred more rupees they left with him as they hurried away. They could scarcely wait for a chance to try the rod's power.

At home they found that their housekeeper did not have supper ready. This gave them an excuse, and, remembering Assad, they flew into a rage. They screamed, "Daughter of Demons, why is our supper not ready? You shall die for this."

The eldest of the six grabbed a sharp knife. With one thrust, he tried to cut the housekeeper's throat.

Luckily his aim was poor. The point of the knife only made a deep wound in the good woman's shoulder. But when she saw the blood, she screamed, "I'll take you to the judge. You shall pay for this well."

"It's only a joke, Woman," the brothers cried then. "Your wound will close. The blood will go away. We have a magic rod that will cure you."

The man drew the green stick gently back and forth across the woman's wound, just as he had seen Assad cure his wife. But, alas, the wound did not close. The blood did not disappear. They had to send for the doctor.

When the houskeeper's wound had been dressed, the six brothers looked at each other. Their faces were long. There was fear in their eyes.

"Tricked again!" they wailed. "What shall we do? The woman will indeed go to the judge. How can we speak to him of a donkey that spits out gold? Of a rabbit that carried a message? And a rod that brings the dead to life? He will never believe we meant the woman no harm."

And the brothers were right. The judge did not believe their tale. He took all their possessions to give to the woman whom they had wounded. And he sent them forever out of that town.

So it was that Assad the Wise had their fifteen hundred rupees for himself. That was indeed a good price for a nanny goat.

THE BIRD AND THE BUFFALO

The bird in this story may be of one kind or another. It depends on the country in which the tale is told. Some say it was a small ricebird or a tickbird which lives on the insects on a water buffalo's back. A few even declare it was a wee hummingbird.

It is easier to believe, however, that it was the long-legged cattle egret. A dark-gray water buffalo with this white bird perched on its back is a common sight in many of the hot countries of Asia.

The water buffalo may be drawing a plow. Or he may be standing, nose-deep, in a stream or canal. Where the sun sends such hot rays down on the earth, what could be better than covering one's body with such cooling water?

The white egret walks up and down on the buffalo's back. He pecks at the ticks and the flies which crawl over its dark-gray hide. Or he takes a nap there in the hottest part of the day.

It was not always like this, so the Philippine grandmothers

tell the children on the island of Mindanao. There was one time, long ago, when the water buffalo grew tired of having an egret always on his back.

The buffalo then tried to drive his unwelcome visitor off. With an angry swish of his tail, he would sweep his back clear. The bird would flap his white wings and fly off into a nearby coconut tree.

You can imagine that the egret was sad to lose his comfortable resting place. He missed his good hunting ground for ticks and flies. So he tried to get back into the good graces of the buffalo.

"I will work harder to keep your back clean of the insects that bite into your hide," the egret promised. "Just let me come back and I will take care not to let my claws dig in too deep."

But the buffalo only tossed his wide-spreading horns. He only swished his long tail the harder.

"Dear Water Buffalo," said the egret. "The good God-Who-Made-All-Things intended that I should rest on your back. He taught us egrets to eat ticks and flies. Where can I find such food so easily as from my perch on your shoulders? It is my right to be there, by the wish of God. Please, dear Water Buffalo, let me come back."

But the buffalo would not. So the egret called to the donkey in the yard around the thatched hut of the beast's owner.

"Is it not the custom, Donkey, that we birds should have perches on the water buffalo's back?"

"Well, I have always seen you birds there," the donkey agreed. "But I myself would not like to have you on my back. So I cannot decide this matter for you."

The egret then lit on one of the broad horns of the buffalo.

There the lashing tail could not reach him. And from that safe perch he argued and argued with the poor buffalo. He talked so much and so long, indeed, that the buffalo at last gave in a little.

"We shall decide the matter by a drinking match," the beast said. He dearly loved to drink water and he always was thirsty. "We shall see which of the two of us can drink the most at one time. We shall go down to the river, and the one who can drink the most shall say whether or not I must let you perch on my back."

The water buffalo thought surely he would win this drinking match. With his great mouth and wide throat, surely he could take larger gulps. And his stomach would hold many, many times more water than would that of the cattle egret. Of course he would win.

The egret knew all this, too. He was a wise bird. But there seemed to be no other means of making the buffalo change his mind. So he agreed to the drinking match. Perhaps he could think of some clever plan to get the best of the buffalo, whose wits were not very quick.

"My friend the donkey here and my master's goat shall be my watchers at the drinking match," the buffalo said.

"I choose as mine the parrot and the mountain eagle." The egret naturally wanted members of the bird race to look out for him.

Now, the home of this buffalo was almost on the seashore. From the top of a tall coconut palm tree on the edge of the river, the egret could see where the river flowed into the ocean. The bird could watch the yellow water of the muddy stream meet the blue waves of the salt sea.

The egret noticed many interesting things from his perch

in the top of the palm tree. And he remembered what he saw. It came to his mind now that sometimes the river water was high between its banks. Sometimes it was low.

The clever bird found that when the ocean water ran up into the river, the riverbed was full. When the ocean water began to flow backward, the river water dropped down. Of course, he did not know anything about ocean tides.

So on this afternoon, when he was seeking a plan to out-wit the water buffalo, the egret sat in the palm tree and thought about this river, where the drinking match was to take place. Patiently he perched there until the tide was high and the river's bed was full. And he noted the exact spot in the sky where the sun stood.

When the ocean water began to run in the other direction and the river began to fall, he again looked at the sun. No doubt it would also begin to fall at almost the same time the next day.

With a satisfied squawk, the white bird flew off to find the gray buffalo. He had thought of a plan by which he might yet get the best of that beast in their drinking match.

"You chose a drinking match," the egret said to the buffalo. "And you named the place where it is to be held. It is I who shall decide at what time of day we shall drink."

Now the water buffalo's mind did not seem to move any more quickly than his clumsy legs. And that was very slowly indeed. He did not suspect a trap. So the time of their drink-ing did not seem important to him.

"Very well," he agreed. "You shall set the time."

Next afternoon the ocean tide was still running up the small river when the bird and the buffalo and their four judges took their places on its banks. The parrot and the eagle chose to

perch in the top of the coconut palm tree. The donkey and the goat stood on the very edge of the river. Each one was bent on seeing that the match should be fair.

The animal judges were contented. But the birds in the top of the palm tree were worried. None of those four thought that the egret could possibly drink as much water as the buffalo.

"The buffalo shall drink first," the egret said, with a look at the sun's place in the sky. No one knew why this suggestion was made. But it was important, as you will see.

"I will go first, if you like," the water buffalo agreed. "But how shall we know which of us drinks the most?" He had not thought much about the drinking match.

"We shall make a mark at the water level here on the bank of the stream," the egret cried. "When one of us has drunk his fill, we can easily see if the water level has gone down. In that way we can tell how much water he has drunk."

With his sharp bill, the bird pecked out a line in the soft earth. And so that he too should have his say, the buffalo deepened the line with his horny hoof.

"Now!" shouted the egret, with a sharp look at the sun. "Now, Buffalo, begin."

The buffalo waded a little way out into the stream. He bent his dark head down, and his spreading horns made dark wing-like shadows on the rippling water. He opened his mouth wide. And he began to drink.

One great gulp he took. Then another! Another and another! His mighty swallows could be heard by the birds up in the palm tree as well as by the donkey and the goat and the other animals watching from the riverbank.

The parrot and the eagle clucked sadly. The donkey's ears

flopped and the goat's whiskers swung from side to side as they shook their heads. How could any bird—even a bird with a long bill like that of an egret—take in as much water as this beast was drinking?

"But the river does not grow smaller." It was the donkey who first noticed that the water was still close to the line they had drawn on the bank.

"No, the water is no lower," the other animals said in surprise. They, too, knew nothing about ocean tides. They had never noticed that there was sometimes more, sometimes less water in every stream close to the sea.

The buffalo could not believe what they said. He had swallowed so much water. But it was true. There was no difference at the level line, which he had himself helped to draw. For the tide was still coming in.

He took a deep breath. Then he gulped down more water. He drank and he drank until his sides were ready to burst.

"I can drink no more," he said at last. His head drooped. For he saw there was no change at all in the level of the water in the riverbed.

"It is your turn now," the great gray beast said to the white egret.

The bird looked at the sun. And he said, "In a few moments, just a few moments. I must find something to eat before I begin to drink." And he pretended to be searching for insects in the grass at the river's edge.

He really was watching the line in the riverbank. And when he saw that the water was beginning to drop, when it was just a feather's width below the line, he cried, "No matter about my food. I will drink now."

Standing with his long legs half hidden in the river, the

clever bird dipped his bill into the water. In and out it went! In and out! Each time the egret took only a tiny sip. And each time his small eyes turned to look at the water falling below the level line.

"Look! Oh, look!" Again it was the donkey who called to the others. "The water is falling. The egret is drinking the river all up."

"True! It is true," the parrot squawked. "The water is far below where it was when the buffalo finished."

It was true, of course. The tide had turned. It was now running out. The ocean water was being sucked back into the sea. It was no longer pushing the river water up in its bed.

Slowly, slowly the bird kept dipping his bill into the river. Slowly but surely, the water grew lower before the eyes of the watchers.

"I do not understand it at all, but the egret has won this drinking match," the unhappy buffalo said at last.

"The egret has won," the four judges declared. All of them were as puzzled as the poor water buffalo. But they had to believe what they saw with their own eyes.

"From now on, then," the egret almost sang in his joy, "from now on, Buffalo, it shall be my right to perch on your back whenever I like. I shall ride with you when you go from one rice field to another. I shall peck my food from your hide when you are standing still. And your long tail shall never swish me away."

That's how it was, and that's how it is today. Sometimes a small brown-skinned herdboy sprawls on the back of his family's buffalo. It is the task of such boys to keep watch lest the useful beast should stray too far from home.

Only then does the white egret flap his wings and fly off.

His squawks are perhaps meant to say to the herdboy, "You do not belong here, Boy. This is my place. It was won for me by my forefather long, long ago at the drinking match between that bird and the buffalo."

How Much For A Shadow?

"One morning, long, long ago, three travelers walked into a faraway Cambodian village. Their heads were shaved bare, and they wore bright-orange robes. They made straight for the marketplace, where crowds of people were gathered, buying and selling."

That is how this story of a water buffalo's shadow always began.

Two of the three travelers were young. They looked scarcely older than boys. And they walked, straight and strong, through the throng moving about between the huge banyan trees.

The third traveler, however, was old. He was indeed very

old. There were deep wrinkles in his yellow-brown skin. His head hung down almost to his chest. It was as if it was almost too heavy for his thin neck to carry. The old man's steps were slow, and his young companions held him up by his arms as they led him to a sitting place in the shade of a banyan tree.

"He is a guru. A Holy One!" a watching child cried out to his mother.

"Aye, he is a guru with two of his students from the temple," the woman replied. "Perhaps this Holy One will pass close to us. Perhaps he will give us his blessing." In the Buddhist land of Cambodia, no one was more honored than an old monk or guru. It was easy to tell that he was a Holy One by his shaved head, his orange robe, and his long string of wooden prayer beads.

"This guru must have walked far," the child's father said to the mother. "His sandals are dusty. He is at the end of his strength."

The man had guessed truly. For the old Buddhist monk was at that very moment saying to his young followers, "I am tired, my Sons. I cannot walk farther. Yet we still have a long road to travel. Go find a farmer. And hire for me a water buffalo. I will ride on his beast's back to the next village, where we shall spend the night."

One of the young student monks went off through the crowd. And soon he returned, followed by a farmer with a dark-gray water buffalo with wide-spreading horns. The beast ambled slowly along, with the farmer guiding its steps with taps of a long bamboo rod.

It was agreed between the guru and the farmer just how many silver coins should be paid for the journey to the next village. The weary old man was lifted up onto the broad back of the gray beast. And the little party set forth.

The farmer, walking beside his buffalo, tapped it now and then to keep it moving along the side of the highway. The two youths in their orange robes walked close to their teacher. First one, then the other, steadied the Holy One as he was jounced about on the lumbering animal's back.

The day was fine. No cloud was to be seen in the bright sky overhead. The sun's burning rays beat down on the road that ran between the rice fields. Now and again the travelers mopped their shaved heads with the ends of their orange-colored robes.

The farmer fared better. He had a thatch of black hair to cover his head and he wore no long robe. Nothing he wore at all, except a thin cotton cloth tied round his middle.

It grew hotter and hotter. At last the old guru called to the farmer to stop.

"I do not feel well, my Friend," he said. "My head goes round and round. I must lie down in some shade."

But there was no shade. No tree was near. Rice fields covered every bit of the earth in this part of Cambodia.

"Let the Holy One lie down in the shadow of your beast," one of the students said to the farmer. He pointed to the patch of dark shade made by the animal as it stood still there on the road.

The poor old monk stretched himself out on the ground. It was good to be out of the burning sun, in the shadow made by the buffalo. His young companions cooled his hot head with their woven straw fans. And he seemed to grow stronger.

After a little, a soft breeze began to blow over the rice

fields. The guru opened his eyes. He raised his head from the ground. He was ready to ride on again.

At last the little party reached the end of that day's journey. And they came to a halt under a big banyan tree in the center of the village.

"One, two, three, four, and five!" The old monk began to count out the number of silver coins which had been set for the use of the buffalo.

"But you must add in the cost of the water buffalo's shadow," the greedy farmer put in.

"Ai! Ai! Who ever heard of anyone asking pay for a shadow?" the old guru cried out. "Not one silver coin will I give you for that. Your beast did no work while I lay down at its side."

"The animal served you by carrying you on its back, Holy One," the farmer said then. "It served you also by giving you shelter from the heat of the sun. You must pay for that service too."

Well, they argued and argued. And, as usual, when two people in Cambodia could not agree, they asked the village headman to judge between them.

In this village the headman was known to be wise. He was used to settling such differences. Everyone said that he was fair and that his judgments were good. He listened now to the tale of the buffalo's shadow, and he heard the ancient monk refusing to pay for any such thing. Then, while all listened, he spoke.

"Before I give you my answer, I will tell you a tale," he said. "I will tell you of something that happened to me. It is the same as the story I have just heard. And yet it is not quite the same."

And this is the story the headman told. It is a second story that comes right in the middle of the first one.

"Some years ago I, too, had to take a long journey. I had walked the whole day. I was hungry and tired. Alas, then I was poor. I had nothing to put into my empty stomach but a small bowl of cooked rice. No bits of fish or curry had I. And no money to buy even the smallest bit of spicy sauce for my rice."

"At the rest house I spent the night outdoors under a tree. And there came to my nose the good smells of the kitchen. The cook was boiling a fine mutton stew for a party of very rich travelers. My mouth fairly watered when I smelled that savory pot, and a splendid idea came into my mind.

"I tied my rice loosely inside a piece of thin cloth. And I carried it quickly to the rest-house kitchen.

"'Good day, Cook,' I said politely. 'Will you allow me to hang this bit of rice over your cooking pot? I am too poor to buy food from you. I have no curry, no bits of fish, not even a bit of sauce to give taste to my small meal of rice. But if, for a time, it might hang in that steam from your stew, it will take on its odor and make it easy to swallow.'

"I thought that the cook had a kind heart. For he granted my favor. When the stew was ready, my rice smelled almost as good as if it had on it gravy right out of the pot. I ate it with pleasure.

"When the sun brightened the sky the next morning, I made ready to go on with my journey. But, to my surprise, the cook stopped me. And I found that although I had thought him to be kind, he was truly a greedy man.

"'You shall not leave this place until you have paid me for

the odor your rice got from my cooking pot.' That is just what he said.

"'But it took nothing at all away from your pot, Cook.' At first I thought he was stupid. 'My rice, it is true, had the good smell of mutton stew. But a smell surely is not a thing to be paid for.'

"The cook would not agree. So the oldest man in that village had to judge between us, just as I must do for you two. And this is what he decided.

"'The travelers who actually ate the mutton stew paid for it with actual money. And that was fair,' said he. 'It is fair, too, that this one who had only the odor of the mutton shall pay for it only with the odor of money.'

"Then, Friends, with one hand he grabbed the greedy cook by the neck. With the other hand he gently rubbed the man's nose with a small sack of silver coins.

"'Smell all you wish, you greedy cook,' he cried out. 'Smell well of this money and you will have the pay due you for the smell of your mutton stew.'"

The headman smiled, and he turned to speak straight to the owner of the buffalo.

"You, Farmer, you shall have the same kind of pay. Yet not quite the same. For actually having ridden your buffalo, the guru should pay you in actual money. But for having made use of the beast's shadow while it stood still, he shall pay with the shadow of money. You shall have all you want of his silver coins' shadows.

"But the sun has now set," he continued, looking up at the western sky. "I cannot wait with you here until it rises again so that I may give you a shadow. A sound and a shadow are both merely reminders of the things that make them. So you shall have the sound of the guru's coins, as much as you wish."

The wise judge seized the unhappy farmer by an ear. With his other hand he shook a small sackful of metal coins close to the man's head. He shook them so hard that one could hear them jingle a buffalo's length away. So much noise did they make that the farmer's head began buzzing like a hornet's nest.

"Stop, O Judge, stop!" the farmer cried out. "Stop! I am satisfied. I am well paid for the shadow of my water buffalo."

He turned the beast round and, with blows of his bamboo rod on its thick hide, he hurried it away.

THE MIRACLE OF THE BEGGING BOWL

As Brahma is the God of the Hindu peoples of Asia, so Buddha is the Great Teacher for millions of Buddhists. Many are the stories that are told about Buddha when he lived on the earth. Some tell how he put on the simple robe of a monk and roamed over the land, teaching men how to live. Or how he often made magic, changing himself into a bird or a beast or even an insect. The Great Teacher took on these different forms when he wanted to act out a lesson in kindness or wisdom.

Like his orange-clad followers, who still live in his temples, Buddha carried a begging bowl. Those who put food in it were sure to be blessed by him. The Holy One was too busy thinking of Heaven to worry about food for himself. A little cooked rice, wet with the buttery oil which the Asians call ghee, was all that he needed. And if someone gave him a bit of fish or meat, it was just that much better for the giver.

It is good to give to others, so the Buddhists believe. The way to Heaven is easier for those who do.

And it is Buddha's own begging bowl, so this story has it, that was the cause of a miracle.

Lucky is the Asian temple which has something that once belonged to the Great Teacher. The golden statues of Buddha, even if they rise high toward the roof, are not so precious as a hair from his head or a bone or a tooth.

It is told that when the Great Teacher died, more than two thousand years ago, his body was burned, in the Indian custom. It was from the ashes of the splendid funeral pyre that bits of his bones and his teeth were taken.

Kings paid large sums for even a small bone. They fought with each other for such precious treasures. The lucky one who won built a splendid temple to hold them. Thousands of pilgrims came to pray before the altars upon which they rested. One of the most famous was a spot where, it was said, a footprint of Buddha could be seen in a rock.

So you can imagine that the wooden bowl, which the Holy One had carried in his own hands, would be a special prize. Buddhist writers say it had traveled far when it finally came to the Indian city of Peshawar. To China, back to India, up to Heaven beyond the sky, and even down under the earth, the bowl went. Kings and demons got hold of it from time to time. But none of these kept it long.

In Peshawar its home was in a temple. Twice each day it was taken down from its altar, which was richly trimmed with silver. It was brought out from behind doors of creamy carved ivory. At high noon and at sunset the temple gongs sounded. Prayers were chanted, and a procession of yellow-robed monks

brought the bowl out into the courtyard. The people waited in silence.

"Make your offerings to the Great Teacher!" the monks would chant. "Whoever can fill his bowl to overflowing will ride with Buddha Himself up into Heaven when at last his time comes." This was the promise they gave.

Always there were crowds of eager pilgrims. The rich and the poor! The good and the wicked!

One man who had grown rich by stealing from his neighbors wanted above all things to succeed in filling the bowl. Perhaps he thought that Heaven would then forget his bad deeds.

So he came, with his traveling elephant loaded with gold and gems. But when he poured these into the holy bowl, somehow they disappeared. No matter what he put in, there were never more than a few copper coins on its bottom. The crowd cried out in wonder.

Next after the wicked rich man, there came a poor family who had nothing to give but a few grains of rice. But, lo, when these were dropped upon the bowl's bottom, they grew to be more and more. Soon they had filled up Buddha's bowl until it ran over.

"Ai! Ai!" cried all the other pilgrims. "These good people please our Master. Their way to Heaven is sure."

Stranger still was the miracle when the army of a certain King came to take the holy bowl, by force, away from its temple. That King was a powerful ruler of a rich land. He had already tried to buy Buddha's bowl from its temple guardians. A small fortune he offered, but of course the good monks would not sell.

"Then if I may not buy, I will take the bowl. I shall bring

a thousand fierce warriors, which no monks can withstand."
This was the message he sent to the temple. And he made
good his threat. There soon arrived at the temple gate a thousand armed men and a troop of war elephants, wagons, and
carts.

What could a hundred yellow-robed monks do against such
an army? With their lives they defended the doors of carved
ivory and the silver altar on which the bowl stood.

But the soldiers brushed the monks aside as if they were
so many flies. They flung open the ivory doors. And they
brought the ancient wooden bowl out to their King.

"Though the bowl is now mine," he said, "I will pay for it
well. I will build a great temple in which it will be safe. It shall
be the greatest treasure of my kingdom." The King hoped in
this way to make up for his taking the bowl by force. He laid
down bags of gold before the monks of the temple. Then he
called out in triumph, "Let my traveling elephant be brought
forward. I myself will carry our prize back to our land."

The huge gray elephant was led forth. With its trappings
of red and gold, the beast made a fine sight. But nobody
cheered. The people of Peshawar stood watching in angry
silence.

The mahout, or elephant driver, brought the great beast to
its knees so that the King could climb up into the howdah,
the little roofed seat on the elephant's back.

Purple and gold were the wrappings that were put around
Buddha's bowl. And red was the cushion upon which it was
set down on the King's knees.

"Rise, Beast!" The mahout gave the call, loud and clear.
But the animal did not move.

"Get up, Lazy One!" the mahout shouted again. This time the

elephant's body swayed to and fro. It seemed to be trying to get itself up on its feet. But it was as if it could not.

"Blessed be Buddha!" shouted the people of Peshawar. "He has turned the legs of the beast to stone." And not until the King had climbed down and the bowl was once more on the temple steps did that elephant rise.

"Bring forth the cart with the four great wheels," the King cried. "Harness to it eight elephants. They surely will be able to make its wheels roll."

But it was again the same story. The elephants' mahouts gave the command: "Pull!"

"Pull! Pull!" cried the King.

Again and again the huge creatures strained their muscles. But the wheels would not turn.

"Blessed be Buddha!" The shout rose again from the yellow-robed monks. "Buddha wills it that his bowl be left in our keeping."

This all happened long ago. So long ago was it that no one now can be sure it happened at all. But on that very spot a splendid temple was built by this King. Some say it was because he was ashamed and because he feared the anger of the Great One. However it was, the new temple was far finer than the one in which he found the bowl. And it stood there in Peshawar for many years. Its lofty tower was a reminder to all pilgrims of how Buddha would not allow his bowl to be taken away.

Whether the bowl is still there today, I cannot tell you. Perhaps it has now been taken by Buddha up into the sky to join him in Heaven. Or perhaps some demon has stolen it and it is with the dragons of the underworld. Who knows? But, wherever it is, it surely still has the blessing of Buddha, who, people say, used it when he was on earth.

THE GRATEFUL BEASTS

In a distant part of Burma there once lived a widow with one son, who was named Woon Daw. When her husband died, she was left to bring up the boy alone. And she tried her best to give him the training which his father would have wished him to have.

"My son," the widow said to him one day, "you are now as tall as a man. You will soon become the head of this household. You will be the owner of all of your father's wealth.

"Now you are a young man. But you do not yet understand the ways of the world. Go forth from this house. Visit the friends of your father. Perhaps they will teach you how to use money wisely." So she gave him a bag of silver coins; and she sent with him three servants to care for him on his journey. And Woon Daw set out to see the wide world.

Now the youth had a kind heart. He remembered well the good rule of Buddha that one should be kind to all creatures. This could clearly be seen when he met, in his travels, a man dragging behind him a weak, sickly dog. The poor creature's tail drooped between its legs. The dog panted and whined.

Woon Daw's good heart was touched. It was clear that the dog's master had not given the animal food for many days.

"Will you sell me your dog, good sir?" Woon Daw said to the cruel man. "I will give you one hundred pieces of silver if you will let me take it and care for it."

One hundred pieces of silver was a great deal of money for such a poor beast. So the man gladly consented.

"Take this dog back to my mother," Woon Daw said to one of the servants who was with him on his journey. "Tell her to feed it well and give it a bed. Bid her care for it until it is fat and strong once again."

The young man's mother was surprised. It seemed strange that any of her husband's friends should have advised Woon Daw to pay one hundred silver coins for such a miserable animal. But she, too, had a kind heart. She cared for the dog well. Soon he became a strong, handsome creature who barked at each stranger who came to her gate.

Not long thereafter Woon Daw met another man on the highway. This one had a meowing white cat, shut up in a basket.

"The cat is not happy in that small basket," Woon Daw said to his servants. "I shall buy this animal also and send it home to my mother."

Who would not sell a cat for a hundred pieces of silver? Of course the cat's owner took it out of the basket and put it into the arms of Woon Daw.

"I cannot think why my husband's friends give my son such bad advice," the widow said when the second servant brought home the cat. It did not come into her mind that it was the youth's own kind heart which had caused him to pay such a large sum for a cat.

Well, a dog and a cat make nice pets. The dog guarded her gate. The cat caught many mice. So having them in her house was not hard for Woon Daw's mother.

It was a different matter with the third animal which Woon Daw sent home. This one was a weasel, a furry wild creature. The youth bought it from a hunter for one hundred pieces of silver.

"How shall I keep this fierce little beast here in my house?" the widow asked herself. "It will be unhappy shut up indoors. It cannot live in the courtyard, for it will eat all our young chickens and ducks. I will put it in a comfortable cage in a shady corner of our back garden."

Each day the good woman took food to the weasel. But it would not eat. It grew thinner and thinner.

One morning a monk, a Holy Man in a yellow robe, knocked at the widow's gate. He held out his wood begging bowl for a bit of cooked rice. And when she brought it back to him full, Woon Daw's mother told the monk of her troubles with her son's unhappy weasel.

"A weasel is wild," the wise old man said to her. "It does not like to be shut up in a cage. You must set it free."

"But my son sent the creature to me so that it might be

safe from the hunters." Woon Daw's mother was troubled. However, she thought she should obey the wise monk.

She set down a bowl of food in the midst of the forest beyond her garden. And as soon as the weasel was set free it began to eat. The little beast ate and ate, and then it ran gaily off through the trees.

The weasel drank at a running brook. Then it curled up under a bush to take a nap.

"I owe my life to Woon Daw," the weasel said to himself when he awoke. "I must repay him somehow."

It happened at his very next drinking place that he found a small shady pool where the daughters of genies were accustomed to bathe. In the clear water, just at the edge of the pool, the weasel saw a yellow glow. With his tiny paw he scooped out a shining gold ring.

"I shall take this ring to my friend, Woon Daw," the weasel decided at once. Somehow or other this little beast knew that the golden ring would work magic for whoever wore it.

"Never take this ring from your finger, Friend," the weasel said to Woon Daw when he had found him and presented his gift. "Whatever you wish for shall be yours so long as you have the ring. But once you tell its magic secret to another person, you will lose it. I warn you."

A magnificent palace with seven fine curving roofs was the first thing Woon Daw wished for. He had no sooner spoken his wish aloud than it was standing before him. Men and maid servants were there to serve the rich food on its banquet table. Gold and silver filled its treasure chests to overflowing.

From all parts of that land people came to wonder at the splendor of the palace of this young man, Woon Daw. Among them was a neighboring King and his fair daughter. So handsome was Woon Daw in his silken robe and his jewels that the Princess fell in love with him. So charming was she that he loved her at once. With a fine feast they were married. And they lived happily together in his palace with its seven fine curving roofs.

All went well at first. The young man had only to make a wish, then turn his magic ring on his finger, and it was granted. Woon Daw spent happy days riding his prancing steeds over the countryside. Everyone honored him. And he loved his dear wife.

That was the trouble. He loved her too well, as you shall read.

While her husband was away from their palace, the hours were long for the Princess. One day there came to the gates of the palace a man dressed in the yellow robe of a Holy Man. Because everyone thought he was a monk, he was welcomed. He was even taken in to talk with the Princess, who engaged him to read to her from his holy books.

A man's clothes do not always tell what he truly is. None in the palace guessed that beneath his yellow robe this man was a thief. Somehow he had learned the secret of Woon Daw's precious ring. And he wanted it for himself.

"Does your husband love you, O Princess?" the false monk asked her one morning when Woon Daw was away from the palace.

"Oh, indeed Woon Daw does love me." The Princess was angry that such a thought should come into anyone's mind. "Woon Daw grants my slightest wish. He loves me above everything in the world."

"Does he sometimes permit you to wear his gold ring, then?"

The face of the wily, would-be monk showed no trace of his plot.

"I never have asked for it," said the Princess. "Why should I wear it? It is his ring."

But when the man in the yellow robe had gone away, the Princess was thoughtful.

"Could it be that my husband would refuse to let me put on his ring? Could it be that he loves that circle of gold more than he loves me?" she asked herself. And this is just what her crafty visitor had meant she should do.

"Woon Daw, let me try your gold ring on my own finger," the Princess said the next day when her husband was making ready to go for a ride. "Let me wear it just this once, while you are gone."

At first Woon Daw refused. But when he saw tears in his beloved wife's eyes, his heart melted.

"You shall wear it," he said as he put it on her finger. "But you must not take it off for any reason at all. And you must not show it to anyone."

Truly the Princess meant to obey his command. But she did want to prove to the man in the yellow robe that her husband loved her above anything else in the world. So she held out her finger with the gold ring upon it, for him to see.

Before she could draw her hand back, the thief had pulled the ring off it. In a wink of an eye he had put it on his own finger. Before her amazed eyes, he made a wish and changed himself into a black crow. With the ring in his beak he flew out of a window and was gone.

The poor Princess and her companions watched the black bird fly far out over the ocean. They saw him make straight for an island in the very midst of the sea.

"We never can reach him there. Oh, what have I done!" The poor Princess wept. In those days, in that country, there was no boat large enough to go so far over the water.

Woon Daw's heart sank when he heard that his ring had been stolen. But when he saw his wife's tears, he could not be angry. He only sent forth the word that his greatest treasure, his golden ring, had been stolen. A rich reward he offered to the one who brought it back to him.

This news came to the cat, the same cat which Woon Daw had befriended. And that cat thought and thought how he could help his dear friend.

"I will go get the ring for Woon Daw," the cat decided. And he left his warm place in the good widow's house and set forth on his quest.

On the way through the woods the cat came to the pool where the genies' daughters bathed. It was the very same pool where the magic ring had been found by the weasel. On this day the cat could see the heads of the fairy girls as they swam about in the cool water. On the edge of the pool there gleamed, in the grass, their shining necklaces of pearls. For safety they had taken them off before they had gone into the water.

Quick as a bird's flight, the cat gathered the necklaces up. Before the genies' daughters could stop him, he had gone off into the bushes to hide them.

"Come back, Cat," they cried. "Without our necklaces we cannot go back to our home. Bring them back to us, please. You shall have your reward."

"Make me a dry path through the ocean to the home of that thief who stole Woon Daw's ring. Then I will show you the hiding place of your pearls."

As if by magic, the waters of the sea parted. The cat ran like lightning along it to the palace of the false monk. Luckily the wicked man was asleep. His hand was dangling over the edge of his bed.

Gently the cat slipped the ring off the man's finger and into his mouth. And away, along the path through the ocean, he fled back to the mainland. The waters closed after him. And, without the magic of Woon Daw's ring, the thief was never able to leave the island again.

"I repay your kindness, my Friend," the cat cried when she brought his ring back to Woon Daw. "And now I would like to live here with you in your palace."

Not long after, the dog brought the message to Woon Daw that his mother, the widow, was dead. And so a place in the palace was made for him, too.

All was happy once more. But there were still in that land thieves who wanted the magic ring for themselves. One night they came in a great band to storm the gate of the palace. They meant to kill Woon Daw and then take his ring from his finger.

It was the dog this time who became the hero of the story. He flew at the throat of the robber chief. Before the eyes of all the other thieves, the dog brought the man to earth. And, of course, then they all ran away.

The next day Woon Daw called together the people who lived in his palace. The Princess was there. Even the guards from the palace gate stood by to hear what their master would say.

The dog and the cat were close to the feet of Woon Daw. And they heard him say as he turned his ring, "I wish that my friend the weasel should be here too."

No sooner were the words spoken than in through the door

came this wild little beast to sit by the side of the two other animals.

"I have called you three here to thank you," Woon Daw began. "Had it not been for this weasel, this cat, and this dog, I should not have this fine palace, this beautiful wife of mine, and my treasure chests full of gold. I want it to be known that there is a place for each one of them in my household. The weasel may like better to have a den in our woods. But that is his choice."

"We did only repay your kindness to us, Master." It was the small weasel speaking. "Your magic wishing ring was only a fitting return for your freeing me from the hunter."

"You paid a hundred pieces of silver to save my life," cried the cat. "It was only right that I should do you a favor and get back your lost ring."

Both the weasel and the cat spoke with quiet modesty.

Not so the dog. He loved his master well. And he was jealous of the other two.

"You saved my life, too, Woon Daw. And I was glad to drive away the robbers who meant to take your ring from you. All three of us have been able to help you. But I think that I, your dog, should have the place of greatest honor in your household. I saved your golden ring at the risk of being killed myself."

Of course the weasel and the cat objected to this. There was a great to-do between them.

"I cannot choose between you," Woon Daw said at last. "I owe each one of you too much. We shall let the Princess decide. Her wisdom is great."

Well, the Princess thought for a time. She held her head in her hands. And then she spoke.

"The cat and the weasel both have given great service. But the dog saved Woon Daw's life from the band of robbers who had come to kill him. Let him have first place in his master's household."

And so it is that in many a household the dog comes first, before the cat or any other animals who have shown themselves to be the friends of man.

Three Silly Schoolmasters

There was a time long ago in the city of Baghdad when there were not enough schoolmasters. Almost anyone then could find positions as teachers of boys. As for the girls, their mothers taught them at home.

The true schoolmasters of Baghdad were wise, as all schoolmasters should be. But some of those young men who were brought in to fill empty places were stupid. They were worse than stupid, indeed; they were silly. They were not proper schoolmasters at all.

Their pupils were already brighter than they. At least this was true of the three teachers in this story, which Ambar, the teller of tales, repeated often in the marketplace.

The three young men were friends. I do not remember just what their names were. We may as well call them, however, Abdul, Selim, and Yusef. As you will see, not one of them had any brains in his head.

Abdul, Selim, and Yusef were sitting, one afternoon, on a

bridge over the River Tigris, in the center of the city. They were watching the boats move back and forth on the waters beneath the bridge.

A fine boat was passing. Its sail was flung high. One could see its rich owner, a merchant in silk gown and turban, sitting in its forepart.

As the splendid vessel slipped under the bridge, its owner looked up. His eyes met the grinning faces of the three young schoolmasters. And he waved them a greeting.

"That is a rich man, indeed," one of the three said to the other two. "To receive a warm greeting from such a one is an honor."

It was Abdul who was speaking. He showed that he thought well of himself when he added, "I feel sure the man's greeting was meant just for me."

"Nay, Abdul," cried Selim. "The merchant was looking at me."

"You are both wrong. His salute was for me, Yusef."

"It was for me, Abdul."

"Surely for me, Selim."

"I know he meant it for me alone." So the argument went. Each one claimed the honor, if in truth it was any honor.

"The only way to decide the matter is for us to ask that rich merchant. He alone knows which of us he meant to greet." All three nodded their silly heads. They rented a small boat and sailed after the merchant down the great river. They sailed upstream, they sailed downstream. They looked hard at each boat they passed. But they did not find the great man they were seeking.

They were still looking when the night came. The wind died down. The sails on their small boat hung limp. They were afraid they would have to spend the whole night on the river.

But somehow they drifted safely to the shore of an island nearby.

There they were lucky. They came upon their rich merchant at the door of his house, which was built on the island.

"Allah be praised, we have found you," they said politely. They bowed as they asked Allah's blessing upon him.

"Allah give thee peace, Strangers," the surprised merchant replied. "What would you have of me?"

"It was we three who looked down from the bridge as you sailed under it this afternoon," Abdul began. "You will remember us, for you honored us with a greeting. We cannot decide which one of us three you were saluting. So we come to you to settle the matter for us."

The merchant laughed. He was about to say that he had waved his hand at many people that day. But he saw that his answer meant much to these silly young men.

He was a kind man. He did not like to hurt any guest's feelings. So he said, "Friends, it is late. You must be hungry. You shall dine with me, and I will give you shelter for the night. And before you go away I will tell you which one of you I was saluting." The man was amused by the simple ways of his guests.

Servants brought forth a great round brass tray, heaped high with rice and roast kid. And the three hungry schoolmasters ate their fill.

Coffee was poured. Then the merchant said to his strange guests, "Now we can talk at our ease. You shall each one tell me a tale. You shall speak of the strangest happening of your whole life. The one who tells the most curious tale will be the one whom I will salute when you depart."

Abdul was first.

"I have only lately become a schoolmaster," he said to the merchant. "My pupils are lively. They like to play tricks. Sometimes they even play tricks upon me.

"Well, one day I had reason to keep them long at their books. So they were not pleased when they went away later than usual. Until several days had gone by, I did not know that they came back once more that evening.

"You see, those boys brought mud blocks back with them. They laid them up in the doorway of the school. One mud block on another. So they filled in the opening. Then they covered those blocks with plaster the very same color as the wall of the school. It was not at all strange that I could not see the door when I came the next day.

"My school had always had a door in its wall. So when I could not find a door, I was sure that this building could not be my own school.

"'Where is our schoolhouse, Boys?' I asked the children who stood round me.

"'Oh, Master,' they replied, 'our schoolhouse has gone away. It must have been angry that you kept us so long at our books yesterday. That is surely why it went away during the night.'

"I looked and I looked for the runaway schoolhouse. But I could not find it. Soon I was thinking the boys had spoken the truth."

The merchant looked hard at Abdul. Surely he must be making a joke. But the young man was not smiling.

"What did you do then, Schoolmaster?" he asked.

"Why, I kept on looking for my schoolhouse, of course. To

each man I met, I said, 'Allah be with you, Friend. Have you seen my runaway schoolhouse?'

"Each man looked at me with surprise. Then he replied, 'Oh, your school must be somewhere, just ahead of you.' But when I reached that place, no school did I find.

"Dark came upon me when I was in the next village. There I met an old man. He had not seen my school, but he offered me shelter for the night. And we went inside his house.

"There another strange thing took place. That old man said to his wife, 'We want some milk. Milk me, Wife, milk me!'

"Now whoever heard of a man being milked?"

Here the merchant broke in. "Perhaps he meant her to bring him milk from the cow."

"They had no cow that I could see. It may be I heard wrongly. But that is how it sounded to me. And the woman soon came back with a bowl of sweet fresh milk in her hand. I drank. It was good—the best milk I ever tasted.

"The next morning I asked the old man again about my runaway school. I told him how the boys had said my school-house had gone off in anger. Then that wise man said, 'Your school has, no doubt, forgotten its anger by now. Go back to where it stood. Look for its door where it used to be. Take off the plaster there, and in the future be more kind to your young pupils.'

"How do you think that old man knew that the door of my school was still under that plaster? I had only to take the mud blocks out of the doorway. It was all just as before.

"But the strange thing is yet to come. That night, being thirsty, I said to my wife, "Milk me, Woman, milk me!" I spoke the words just as I had heard the old man. But my wife thought I had gone out of my mind. She pulled at my fingers as if she was milking a cow. But no milk came. That old man must have had some other secret which he did not tell me. One day I shall go back and ask him what it was."

The merchant laughed out loud. Then he nodded to Selim that he might tell his tale.

"I also am a schoolmaster, a very new one," Selim said to the merchant. "And I have had an even stranger thing happen to me.

"Everyone knows that a sneeze makes a man weak and gives the bad spirits power to harm him. So I have taught my pupils what they should do whenever a sneeze comes from someone who is near them. From me they have learned to hold out both hands and call on Allah to protect him who has just sneezed.

"Well, one day my pupils came running to find me. 'Master,' they cried, 'down inside the well by the school there are boys who look just like us. Are they new pupils? Will they, too, learn their lessons from you?'

"I hurried out with my boys to look down into the well. Sure enough, in the dark shining water, I saw the faces of boys. Their teacher was there too. And he looked like me.

"Oh, I was angry. How dared another schoolmaster bring his pupils to my school? How dared he put them down there in my well?"

Here the merchant broke in. "But surely you know, Selim, that water is like a——" He did not finish his sentence. He did not say "like a mirror" because Selim was not listening to him. The silly young fellow was going on with his story.

"I shook my fist at that schoolmaster. He shook his fist back at me. I called to him, 'Go away!' And out of the well came the same words: 'Go away!' Everything I did or said that man did the next minute."

"Selim does not know about an echo either," the merchant thought to himself.

"I was so angry I decided I would go down into the well. I would drag out that schoolmaster and his boys. I climbed into the bucket. I told my pupils to let its rope down slowly and gently.

"All would have gone smoothly, but it was cold in the well. Alas, I sneezed, and at once the boys let go the rope. They stretched out their hands and called out, 'Allah protect thee!' And, of course, I fell out of the bucket and into the water.

"But—you'll be surprised, Merchant—there was no other schoolmaster but me in that well. There were no strange boys either. I cannot think where they could have gone."

The merchant thought Selim must surely be making a joke. He could not believe that a teacher of boys would not know that a well is like a mirror. How could he not have seen that the face there was his own? How could he not know that the words he heard were his own words, coming back in an echo?

But Selim's face had no smile. His eyes were big with his wonder at this strange happening.

Then it was the turn of Yusef, the third of these silly schoolmasters.

"I have a wife, Merchant," he began his strange story. "She is a terrible woman. She has a sharp tongue, a tongue sharp as a knife. I am afraid of her, I tell you.

"My wife has some hens which lay eggs for our breakfasts. She guards her eggs well. She does not let me touch them without asking her, no matter how hungry I am.

"One day my wife went out to the marketplace to do some shopping. I truly was hungry, and so I went to the cupboard. And I took two of her eggs. I thought I would cook them before she came home and she would not know.

"But before I could break those eggs into a pan, I heard my wife's footsteps. There was I, near the door, with the two eggs in my hand. I had no good place to hide them, so I popped them into my mouth. One egg went into my right cheek. One went into my left cheek. Luckily their shells were firm. But my face looked as swollen as if a bee had stung me on both sides.

"'What is wrong with you, Husband?' my wife cried when she saw my face.

"With the two eggs in my mouth, of course, I could not speak. I was so afraid of her that I began to shake. I fell flat on the ground.

"Straightway my wife sent our son for the doctor.

"'Open your mouth,' that doctor said the very first thing. I shook my head. I held my lips tight together. I did not speak because then the eggs would have rolled out on the floor.

"'We must cut those lumps out of this man's face at once,' the doctor said. I shook my head again and again. But he paid no attention. He took out his doctor's sharp knife, and he slit my cheeks open. I was right. My wife was in a fury when she saw the two eggs pop out."

The merchant could scarcely believe his own ears.

"You let the doctor cut open your cheeks?" he asked in amazement. "You said nothing at all? Why did you not just spit out the eggs?"

"No, I said nothing," Yusef answered. "You see, I knew how angry my wife would be."

"Well, this is the strangest tale I ever have heard." The merchant was still shaking his head. "You are the one, Yusef! Let us say it was you to whom I gave greeting under the bridge this afternoon. And to you I shall give a special salute when you three go away from my house in the morning."

As he stood on his doorstep to say good-bye, the merchant made a bow to each of his guests. Then he made a second and deeper bow to Yusef. He laughed for three days after the three silly schoolmasters had gone on their way.

THE CLOUD HORSE

A heavenly white horse, with shining black mane and tail, is the hero of this story of ancient Ceylon. In the beginning—so it is told—part of this large island, off the southernmost tip of India, was the homeland of man-eating demons called Rakshasas. The good people, the humans, were to come later.

In those fairy-tale times, things were not always as they seemed. Animals took on the forms of men. Men became animals. There was little difference between them.

The heavenly white horse with the shining black mane and tail spoke with the words of men when he flew down out of the clouds. It was this Cloud Horse who saved Vijaya, the first human to land upon Lanka, from the man-eating Rakshasas.

To understand about Vijaya, one must first know about his famous grandfather, Sinha the Lion. Some people say Sinha—whose name was the same as "lion" in the ancient speech—was indeed an animal, with shaggy mane and tawny paws. Others think the name "Sinha" was given to him because he was

as brave and strong as a lion. But all agree that Sinha, the Lion
King, was the forefather of all the humans who came later to
live on this island in the Indian Ocean.

Sinha's wife was a human Princess, a lady of beauty and
goodness. Their two children, and also their thirty-two grandsons, were strong and good to look upon. Of these last, Prince
Vijaya was the oldest and the one who gave Sinha the most
trouble. He and his friends played bad jokes on the good
people of Sinha's kingdom in India. So wild were their pranks
that many complaints were brought to the King.

"Send your grandson, Vijaya, and his bad company away
from this land, we pray you, O Sinha." The merchants came in
a body. "They take what they like from our houses without
paying. They torment our families. We have no peace."

Again and again Sinha scolded Vijaya. But the young Prince
and his followers paid no attention. And there came a day when
the lot of them were put on a ship and sent out to sea.

"You may sail where you like, Vijaya," the Lion King said as
he bade his grandson farewell. "But you may not come back
here until you have learned how to live as a royal Prince
should."

For many days that ship, filled with the wild young men,
sailed over the ocean. And it was during its wanderings that
wisdom from Buddha came to Vijaya. Gone now was his wish
to torment and tease, or to do even worse things. By the time
the ship brought him to Lanka, Vijaya was as well mannered
as the best of princes in the Lion King's country.

It had been many days since Vijaya and his friends had seen
land. Their food was all gone. Their drinking water was only
the few drops of rain which they caught in bowls on their
ship. They were weary with being tossed about on the sea.

And they scarcely could make their way over the sandy beach to the city of the Rakshasas.

"Welcome, Strangers, welcome!" These were the cries which greeted Vijaya and his friends. They came from Rakshasas who had put on the forms of beautiful women. Clad in bright silks, and with red lotus blooms in their black hair, they welcomed the strangers with sweet smiles and gay songs.

"Our husbands have long been lost at sea," the Rakshasa women told their guests. "Three years and more ago they sailed away, and they have not come back to us. You are here without wives. We have no husbands. We welcome you into our houses."

Of course this was not true. The Rakshasa men were in hiding. They were waiting only until their women should have the humans within their power. Then they would come forth and there would be a fine feast for these man-eating demons.

Vijaya and his friends had no thought of danger. The Rakshasas' city looked just like cities in India. In the country nearby there were cattle and goats. Dogs played in the door-yards of the comfortable houses. How should these strangers guess that these gentle, smiling women were demons who wished to devour them?

"You shall dwell with me in my house," said one after another of the Rakshasas to a young man she had chosen. And the youths consented.

It was a brass lamp, shining in the darkness of the night, which told Vijaya the truth. Its light fell full on his hostess, who had become her real self as she slept. Instead of a fair smiling face, Vijaya saw a demon with long teeth and wrinkled skin.

"Take care, Vijaya!" The voice came from the gleaming lamp. "Go quickly away from this demon land. The Rakshasas are just waiting to put you in prison until they can devour you."

What god was it that protected the humans from these evil beings? The tale does not tell. But the warning was heeded.

Next morning Vijaya called his friends to gather about him on the seashore. But, alas, their ship was gone, sent out to sea or hidden away by the Rakshasas.

"How shall we get away from this land?" Sinha's grandson lifted his arms to the sky and prayed for help from the gods.

It was then that the clouds parted and the heavenly horse appeared over their heads. White as a pearl was his coat. Black as a crow's shining feathers were his mane and his tail.

Like the wind, the Cloud Horse crossed the sky toward the demon island. Like a falling leaf, he dropped swiftly upon the beach beside Vijaya.

"I will save you, Grandson of Sinha." The Cloud Horse spoke with words which Vijaya and his friends could understand. "I will save your friends as well. Jump on my back! Take hold of my mane and my tail! Whoever can grasp even one of these hairs shall be carried to safety off this island.

"But listen well!" the Cloud Horse warned them. "Once we are in the air, no one of you must look back. He who so much as turns his head at the cries of the Rakshasas will lose his chance to escape. I can then do nothing more to save him."

The words had scarcely been spoken when the demon women, again beautiful in their human forms, came running down to the beach. At the sight of them, the Cloud Horse neighed liked the thunder. Fire like the lightning spurted out of his nostrils. With slashing hoofs, he galloped upon the Rakshasas; and they fled back to their homes.

"Quick, now! Take your places! We must be gone before the demons come back." The Cloud Horse stood still while Vijaya

leaped onto his silvery back. Others jumped up beside the Prince. And those who could not find a place to sit grasped the black mane and the long tail of the heavenly steed.

All would have been saved, but the Rakshasas were there again on the seashore. They were weeping and calling, "Come back! Come back! Oh, dear Friends, come back!"

There were foolish youths in Vijaya's company who forgot the words of the Cloud Horse. They turned their heads when they heard the voices of the fair women. And at once they were falling, down, down into the sea.

In long log canoes the Rakshasas came out to get them. And before the young men knew what had happened, they were thrown into prison. There they would wait until they were needed for the demons' feasting.

How Vijaya came back later to Lanka is another story. He must have brought with him all of his brothers, the thirty-one other grandsons of Sinha the Lion. No doubt he had also a great army of warriors to help him destroy the Rakshasas. Perhaps they all crossed the ocean between India and Ceylon on the Monkey Bridge there. It was Vijaya, so the old people say, who made the fair green island country a fit home for man.

Soon ships from faraway lands were bringing merchants to Vijaya's island to buy sweet sandalwood and spices from its thick forests. Others came to get the sapphires, the rubies, the emeralds, and the other gemstones which lay in its earth.

"Country of Lions" is the meaning of "Sinhala," the name that was now given to the former Lanka. So there may just be some truth in this old legend about the first settlers of this land, whose people today call themselves "Sinhalese."

A BRIDE FOR THE SEA GOD

A certain city of fisherfolk once stood on the shores of the island country of Ceylon. No means of earning their living had most of the people there except by taking fish out of the ocean.

Of course, there were those who served the King in his palace, and those who sold to the fisher families their food and their clothes.

But every day from this city, there went forth many fishermen in their narrow, log, sailing canoes. Then, as today in Ceylon, each boat was fitted with an outrigger. This was a log which floated alongside, fastened to the canoe with wooden arms. The outrigger helped the long narrow boat to stay right side up in the rolling waves.

Some men who did not fish built boats for their neighbors. Others made the strong nets which brought the fish out of the sea.

The women, of course, kept house for the fishermen. They cooked their families' food and took care of their clothes.

So it is easy to understand that the sea was important to these fisherfolk. When the waters were calm, fish filled their nets. Then they gave thanks to the mighty Sea God who, they said, ruled the waves. When times were bad and storms swept over the ocean, even the outriggers could not keep the canoes safe. At such times fish were few and all in the land were hungry.

The people of that Ceylon city, then, were sure the Sea God was angry. They threw wreaths of flowers upon his waves. They gave him rich gifts. Sometimes they even sent out, in a royal canoe, a fair young girl to be the bride of the Sea God.

This is the story of just one such bad time in ancient Ceylon. Truly it was a time of great trouble. The winds blew without stopping. Mountain-high waves rose out of the ocean, and the water rolled over the land, far in from the seashore.

For days and for weeks it was like that. It was not safe for the fishing boats to put out from their landing places. No fish were caught.

The priests from Buddha's temples knelt on the seashore. They beat upon their brass gongs. They prayed to the Sea God to forgive whatever the people of the city had done to make him so angry. But the storm did not go away.

At last the King of the city called for Maha Pandit, the wisest soothsayer in all Ceylon.

"What shall we do, O Maha, Wise One?" the King asked. "How shall we please the God of the Sea so that he shall calm the waves?"

"His anger is great, O King," the soothsayer replied. "Only

a fair young bride will make him happy once more. Only then will he bid his waves to be still."

Like everyone else, the King knew of this old custom out of the past. He remembered how a young girl was set adrift in a royal canoe to sail alone out on a stormy sea. What became of such a bride no one knew. Perhaps the canoe was overturned in the midst of the storm. It always was said she had gone straight to the undersea palace of the angry God of the Sea.

This King had a kind heart. He would never willingly give the order that any girl in his country should thus be sent to the undersea kingdom. He had a daughter himself, whom he dearly loved.

So, on this dreadful day, he tried to find an easier way to please the angry God of the Sea.

"Will not a goat, or a buffalo, or some other fine, fat animal serve instead of a girl as a gift for the Sea God?" he asked.

But Maha Pandit was firm.

"One hundred people died of hunger in this city yesterday," he told the King. "The storm must be stopped. The Sea God must have his bride. Your people demand it."

The good King was sad. But there was greater sorrow in store for him.

"No ordinary bride will please the God of the Sea," the soothsayer declared. "She must be the fairest. She must be the most noble in all this city. And that one, O King, is your own daughter, the Princess Sokari."

How could a father send his own daughter on the terrible voyage in a royal canoe? The sharks might break its outrigger and pull her into the sea, even before she could find the palace of the Sea God.

"Would it not be more fair if the bride for the Sea God

should be chosen by drawing lots? Would not some other fair maiden please him as well?" The King made one more try to save his dear daughter.

But Maha Pandit shook his head. "None other than the Princess Sokari can save this land," he replied.

A messenger was then sent into the women's part of the palace. There he knelt at the feet of the King's daughter.

"You are to put on the dress of a royal bride, Princess," he said to her. "You are to wear all your jewels—your sapphires, your rubies, your emeralds, and your pearls. The bridal chair will be waiting for you when the sun again is high in the sky."

Sokari was puzzled. "Does my father, the King, himself send me this message? Has a bridegroom been chosen for me?"

"Aye, a bridegroom has been chosen." The messenger dropped his eyes to hide his tears. "A God is your bridegroom— the God of the Sea! You only can calm his anger so that the storm shall be ended and this land be saved."

The poor Princess grew pale. She, too, knew about the sea brides of other times of great trouble—how they were sent out alone on the sea and never heard from again! But she was a King's daughter. She must not show fear. She would make ready her bridal dress.

There were cheers all through the city when Sokari was carried in the red and gold bridal chair down to the seashore the next day at noon.

"Sokari! Sokari! Sokari will save our children from dying of hunger!" The shouts of the crowd drowned out the music of the gongs and the temple bells.

The ministers were on the seashore to welcome her. They hung bright flower wreaths around her neck, while her father stood watching, with tears rolling down his pale cheeks.

Then a strange thing happened. Suddenly the clouds were gone from the sky. The sun showed its bright eye, and the wind of the storm became a gentle breeze.

"Father! My Father!" Sokari looked for help toward the King.

"It is the will of our people, my dear One; I have no choice," he replied sadly.

There was music and dancing. The priests sprinkled drops of the holy oil from the temple upon the girl's shining black hair. Her jewels sparkled in the bright sun. Her arms shone with their bracelets of red gold. Sokari that day was a magnificent bride.

In the vast crowd on the seashore there was one other whose heart was as heavy as that of the King. This was a handsome young fisherman whose name was Kusa.

When they were children, Kusa had played with the little Sokari on the white sandy beach. He had brought her curious shells. He had built her sand palaces. And he loved her dearly. Not just because she was a pretty child, but because she was so gentle and kind.

Now that they were grown up, Kusa knew well that a fisher youth might not seek the company of a King's daughter. So he had loved her from afar. In this land of Ceylon many young men admired this fair Princess. But none loved her so deeply as this young fisherman.

On the day of her wedding to the Sea God, Kusa stood close to the royal canoe. Gay streamers of silk and long ropes of flowers were twined round its mast. Then Sokari, tied into her red and gold chair, was lifted aboard.

"The storm wind has died. The waves are calm to receive the bride of the sea," the people shouted. It was true. A gentle breeze filled the red sail of the bridal boat as it drifted easily off the beach and out to sea.

Long after the red sail was gone from sight, Kusa stood looking toward the place where it had disappeared.

"Sokari! Dear Sokari! O God of the Sea, be kind to Sokari," he prayed.

Then it was as if Kusa had suddenly made a decision. He ran swiftly back to his father's house. There he filled one jar with fresh goat's milk, another with soup, and a third with cooked rice. Some straw sleeping mats he lifted up on his back. And, so loaded down, he made his way again to the seashore.

Quickly, in the twilight, he set the jars and the mats inside his father's seagoing canoe. He spread its sail; then he pushed it out upon the sea.

Kusa knew the wide ocean well. With the stars as his guides, he steered his boat toward the spot where Sokari had disappeared.

It was three full days, however, before he spied the red sail of the royal canoe. Each time the sun now rose into the sky, he cursed its hot rays. He prayed that Sokari would not be struck down by their burning heat.

"God of the Heavens," he cried out, "send clouds to cover the sun and soften its heat. Sokari must not die before I can reach her."

The good youth's prayer was answered. When, at last, he boarded the bridal canoe, his Princess still breathed. True, she lay on its bottom as if she were dead. But when he bathed her face with the fresh water, which had been put on her boat, she opened her eyes. When he poured drops of the goat's milk between her dry lips, she moved her head weakly to look up into his face.

"I know you. You are the fisher boy, Kusa." Sokari's voice was hardly loud enough to be heard. She was near the end of her strength. But a smile showed on her lips. "How is it, my old Friend, that you are here with me in the midst of the sea?"

"I could not let you go to your death, Princess—not even for the Sea God," he cried. From the tender look in his eyes, the King's daughter guessed that he loved her. He must love her even more than his own life, she thought. Surely he must know that he would be put to death as soon as it was found out that he had cheated the Sea God of his bride.

Gently Kusa lifted the girl into his own boat. The royal canoe was set adrift on the waves. And never again was it found. Perhaps the God of the Sea himself pulled it down to his kingdom.

In a small cove, Kusa found a safe hiding place for their boat. It was better, he said, that they should not return to the city at once.

"Soon the great storm and the anger of the Sea God will be forgotten," he told Sokari. "Soon there will again be plenty of fish. The bad time will be over, and you will be strong again. Then it will be safe for us to go home."

Like a brother the good youth cared for the Princess. When the soup and the goat's milk and the cooked rice were gone, he caught fish in his net to give them the food they needed. Each day Sokari was stronger. Each day, from a lookout in a coconut tree on the shore, Kusa saw more fishing boats.

"It is safe for us now, Princess," he said at last. "We can go home."

Kusa had reasoned well. In that Ceylon city, then, those who had been hungry had now been fed. The ocean waters were calm day after day. The Sea God was sending the fish into the nets. The people were happy.

Only in the palace the lonely King still wept for his dear daughter. He could not forgive himself for sending her away alone on the ocean. And at night he could not sleep.

So it was that the King was awake one day at dawn when Kusa knocked on the palace gates. He could hardly believe his ears when he heard his daughter's own voice calling, "Father, here is Sokari, come home again."

The King himself pushed the guards aside and threw open the gates.

"Daughter! Dear Daughter! The Sea God has sent you back to me!"

"Not the Sea God, dear Father. It is this fisher youth, Kusa, who saved me from the sea." With a grateful and loving look, Sokari pulled Kusa forward to stand by her side.

How happy the King was while he listened to the tale of this brave youth and his bold journey! The people of the whole city were glad, too, when they heard of Sokari's return.

"The Sea God is angry no longer, my people," the King declared to the crowds which gathered outside the palace. "The Sea God has taken our storms away. More fish than ever swim into our nets. It was the God himself who sent Kusa to save our Sokari and bring her back safely."

"Kusa! Brave Kusa!" Now the cheers of the crowds were all for the young fisherman.

"The Sea God has chosen Kusa, instead of himself, to be my husband." Sokari's voice rang out loud and clear. "Out there on the sea I learned to love this youth well. He is strong. He is kind. No royal Prince could be braver than my bridegroom, my Kusa."

The simple fisher youth could scarcely believe his good fortune. All through the wedding feast, while the gongs were sounded and the bells rang, he gave thanks to Heaven. And he vowed that as the son-in-law of the King he would do his duty well.

Kusa kept his vow. So greatly was he beloved that he was himself made King when his wife's father died. Far and wide he was known for his wise commands. And the first order he gave, when he became King, was that never again should a fair young Ceylon maiden be sent out alone on the ocean to be the bride of the Sea God.

THE UNGRATEFUL TIGER

One fine morning, long ago, an orange-robed monk left his temple on the edge of a teak forest in the country of Vietnam. In those ancient times, the land had another name, but no one uses it now.

The morning sun was showing its bright face over the tree-tops. Then, as now, with each sunrise, the Buddhist monks, in their orange robes, went forth from the temples with their begging bowls in their hands. No food would they eat that day except the rice and the fish which the village folk would have ready for them.

The sandaled feet of this monk took him along a narrow

road which ran close to the teak forest. So close it was, indeed, that he could see the monkeys in the trees. He could hear the jackals and other wild creatures moving in the low bushes.

The good monk had not gone very far when he heard a strange noise. It was a whining and groaning, and it came from the forest nearby.

"Some poor beast is in trouble," the monk said to himself. "Those are never sounds made by a man."

He took a few steps along a trail that led into the deep woods. Then he stood still. In the distance he had caught sight of the yellow coat of a tiger.

"Kong Kop!" he whispered. He spoke this name for the king of the jungle under his breath. No one in that ancient land dared speak a tiger's name out loud. The fierce hungry beast might hear. Then it would come and carry him off.

The monk took a few slow steps in the direction of the whining tiger. Then he stood still once more. On his daily walks he took care never to enter the teak forests, for fear of just such wild beasts.

But his Master, the Great Buddha, teaches that all living things must be treated with kindness. One must never, never take the life of any creature. This good monk even drank water through a thin cloth. Only in that way could he be sure that he might not swallow some insect which might have dropped into his cup.

"He who saves a life shall have his reward in Heaven." The monk remembered Buddha's promise. So he did not turn and run away at the sight of the tiger. He knew well that one blow of Kong Kop's mighty paw could take his own life. But this tiger was clearly ill. He might even be dying there on the ground.

"What will be will be," the monk said to himself. "I will see what can be done for Kong Kop."

"How can I help you, Friend?" He stood close, now, looking down upon the weak beast.

"There is no help for me. I must die," the tiger said in a whisper. "Not looking at the ground, I laid myself down on the very hole of a serpent's den. And that serpent has bitten my leg. His poison has entered my body. Yes, I must die."

Now in those long-ago times, people said the Great Teacher used to lend his magic power to those who would do a good deed. Surely it must have been Buddha who put into that monk's mind what he should do.

"Show me your wound, Friend," he said to the tiger. "I will take the serpent's poison away."

Oh, the holy man had courage. He himself sucked the poison out of the tawny beast's body. And soon the tiger rose up onto his feet. He was as strong and as fierce as before the snake had bitten his leg.

Once well again, that tiger forgot he owed his life to this man in the orange robe. He bared his teeth in a snarl. And he cried out, "Foolish man, how dared you come here into my jungle? Do you not know that any creature who enters this forest is my rightful prey?"

"But I came only to save your life." The monk could not believe the tiger would be so ungrateful.

"Still it is my right to kill you and eat you. And that I mean to do."

"Oh, Kong Kop," begged this Holy One. "Have you no thanks for me in your heart?"

"What are thanks when one is hungry? I need meat. You are here. I shall certainly eat you."

"First, then, let us follow the custom of our land." The monk was trying to gain time and to save himself perhaps. "Let us ask others to judge this matter for us. If any one of those we consult says you are wrong, then you shall let me go."

What the tiger thought then, this story does not tell. But since such judging was indeed the custom all through the Far East, he did agree.

The first one asked to judge between the tiger and the monk was a huge water buffalo. He listened to them in silence.

"I saved the tiger's life. I took the poison from his body into my own mouth. Now he wants to kill me." So the holy man told it.

"It is my nature to eat man. This one came into my forest. I say it is my right to kill him." So spoke the ungrateful tiger.

The water buffalo looked long and fearfully at the tiger.

"If I decide against Kong Kop," he was thinking, "he will eat me instead of the monk." So he said aloud, "The holy man was foolish to enter the kingdom of the Lord Tiger. Kong Kop should have his way."

These words brought fear to the monk's heart. But he said, "This is only one judge. Let us ask a second one what we should do." And they sought out a jackal who watched from under a bush.

"How do you judge, Friend?" the monk asked. "Does the tiger have the right to kill me who saved his life?"

The jackal's bright eyes were fixed on the fierce fangs of the tiger. "Kong Kop is stronger than I who must live in his forest. I dare not say no to him," he thought.

"The holy man was wrong. Kong Kop has the right to eat him if he likes." When the jackal had spoken, he crawled far back into his den. He was ashamed. He knew his judgment was unfair.

Next they put the matter before a big monkey who sat in a tree just over their heads.

"Men like this monk forget when a favor has been done for them." The monkey cocked his head on one side. "It was so with my grandfather. He once saw a man fall into an elephant trap. That man could not climb out of the hole until my grandfather reached down his long arm and gave him a pull. But do you think that man was greatful?" The monkey shook his fist.

"No," he went on. "The very next time he went hunting, that man killed my poor grandfather and put him into his cooking pot. No, Holy Man, I say no. Let Kong Kop have his way!"

A vulture nearby was making a meal of a dead squirrel. It was he who was chosen to be a fourth judge. When the great bird heard the tale, he thought of himself at once.

"If the tiger kills and eats up this man, he will never gnaw his bones clean. There will be fine bits of meat left for me when Kong Kop has eaten his fill." So the poor monk once again heard the awful sentence, "The tiger has the right on his side."

"Let us go to the Nat's tree by the side of this road," the monk said then to the tiger. This was a tree, known far and wide, as the home of a spirit—or, as the people of Vietnam called him, a Nat.

In those days Nats often spoke aloud to men. They told men when they were pleased with the presents which they laid at the foot of the tree. They scolded men when they were not pleased at the noise of their hunting.

On this morning the Nat sounded angry. "I do not like men. Yesterday some came and cut off my tree's branches with their

sharp knives. I do not care what happens to any man. Let the tiger kill and eat this one. It is his right."

Now the heart of the good monk was like a stone in his breast. How could he escape from Kong Kop if none of the judges would help him? Well, he would try just once more. He would ask the brown rabbit who was hopping down the forest path.

Everyone said that the rabbit was clever. Perhaps help might come from him.

"You well know, O Rabbit, that Buddha tells us to be kind to each other. I came into Kong Kop's forest only to save his life. Now he would reward me by eating me for his dinner. Is that fair, I ask you? The buffalo and the jackal, the monkey, the vulture, and the Nat of the tree have all decided against me. I surely shall die if you do not see that justice is done."

The rabbit nodded his head. His long ears waved as he said, "You speak true words, Holy Man. One must return good for good." He had already decided to help this orange-robed monk. But he, too, had his eyes on the fierce fangs of the tiger.

"Before I can say who is right, I must see for myself just how it all happened," the rabbit said. "Let us look at the serpent's hole. Let the snake crawl down into it as before."

For all he was so strong and so fierce, that tiger could not have been very bright. For he laid himself down over the mouth of the snake's hole. He even allowed the snake to bite him once again. And a second time the deadly poison flowed into his veins.

Kong Kop whined. Then he groaned. But the holy man made no move to take the poison away.

Well, that was the end of the ungrateful tiger. And it is the end of this story, except for the parting words of the rabbit.

"Go quickly away from here," he told the monk in the orange robe. "Did you not know that there is no mercy to be found in a tiger? Kong Kop is ungrateful by nature. Another time you would do better to save your kindness for some creature with a more thankful heart."

THE BLUE CAT

On a faraway island of Indonesia there once was a King who loved cats. By day and by night he kept a cat by his side. And each one of his pets was more beautiful than the last.

At the time of this story, the King's favorite cat was white. It was an animal with soft, long, silky fur, with tufts of white on its pointed ears and white puffballs covering its toes.

A collar of gold and rubies circled the neck of the King's white cat. A long, fine, golden chain joined the animal fast to his master's wrist. A silken cushion was laid for it at the feet of the King's throne.

Now and then the royal pet would be lifted up into the lap of its master. Some said that the King talked to his cat about the affairs of state. It was well known that those to whom the cat took a dislike were sent away from the court.

Since a king usually sets the fashion for his people, every house on that island sheltered a cat. You can imagine how many there were. Indeed, sometimes it was hard to walk along the streets of the King's city without stepping on some furry beast. People talked about cats from morning until night, and no child had a softer bed or finer food than the family cat. The King liked it that way.

So one can understand how it was that he often saw cats in his dreams.

One morning the chief soothsayer was called before the King. This wise man could read dreams as if they were books. It was to him the King turned when he could not himself guess what his dreams meant.

"Last night, Soothsayer," he said on this morning, "I had a wonderful dream. I dreamed of a blue cat. Oh, the cat was as blue as a bright-blue sky. It had green-yellow eyes, and it wore a collar of rubies just like the one around the neck of my white cat. It lay on my lap as I sat on my throne. People, many people, came bringing me gifts. And such rich gifts as I never have had before. Everyone smiled and was happy. It was surely a sign that a blue cat would bring me good luck.

"But then the blue cat jumped down out of my lap. It ran from the palace. And all those rich gifts disappeared. The smiling people were no longer there. Soothsayer, tell me what my dream can mean."

The old reader-of-dreams, in his soothsayer's robe, knew he must think up a story to please the King. And at once he was ready.

"Your dream truly was wonderful, O King. It tells of great joy for this kingdom. A blue cat will bring riches. A blue cat will bring smiles of happiness for all who live on our island.

"In your dream the blue cat went away. And your treasures went with it. A blue cat must be found to bring back that good fortune."

Now this was a wicked story for that soothsayer to tell the King. He told it so well that the King was sure he was speaking words of wisdom sent down from Heaven. But who ever saw a blue cat—a cat blue as a bright-blue sky? Not you or I— nor that soothsayer either.

But the King did not question what the soothsayer said.

"Let a blue cat be brought to me!" He gave the command. "A cat as blue as the bright-blue sky it must be. And let it quickly be found."

Everyone looked for a blue cat. In palaces and in huts. In garrets and in cellars. By day and by night. Cats out on the streets were caught in traps made of bags. Saucers of milk were set out on each doorstep for any wandering strange cat.

White cats and black cats there were. Gray cats and orange cats. Spotted cats of many colors. But not one blue cat was found.

The King offered splendid rewards. Greater and greater rewards did he promise. At last he even offered to give his daughter in marriage and half of his kingdom to that young man who should find the blue cat of his dreams.

Even that did not succeed at first; and so the King made threats. Each day, when no blue cat was brought to him, he would throw ten of his good people into the palace prison. These unlucky ones were chosen by drawing names out of a bag.

There was fear all through the island then. Nobody smiled. Everyone worried lest his name should be drawn for the prison next time.

The King was growing more and more impatient. He had forgotten entirely that he had a handsome white cat for a pet. That white cat was lonely on its silken cushion on the foot of the royal bed. When, one day, it disappeared, the King did not even ask where it had gone.

Now, in that island country, there was a noble youth who had long had a secret love for the Princess. When he heard how the King had promised her hand in marriage to the finder of a blue cat, he began to think. He thought and he thought. And at last it was he who brought the King his blue cat.

This was a cat which reminded some in the palace of the King's former white favorite. This blue cat was the same size. It had green-yellow eyes. But, of course, its fur was bright blue. Nowhere had there ever been seen such a blue cat.

But the King did not ask questions. Surely this must be the cat of his dream. When he woke that fine morning, there was, on the pillow at the foot of his bed, the blue cat with the green-yellow eyes. Just as in his dream, it was wearing a collar of rubies like the one his white cat had had.

Purring, the blue cat rubbed its head on the King's shoulder. It was truly as if the animal had been his pet for a long time. When the King sat on his throne, the blue cat settled itself on his knees as if it belonged there.

The King now was happy. The people were happy too. Their fear of prison was gone. So they brought many rich gifts to lay at the feet of the King. It was just as long a procession as the one in his wonderful dream.

"I have promised that the finder of my blue cat shall marry my daughter. Let the wedding take place!" And so it was that the noble youth gained his beautiful Princess and the promise of half a kingdom.

But in secret people wondered about the King's blue cat. Some said it was not a blue cat at all. They declared it was only the King's former white pet, whose long silky fur had been dyed a bright blue. Many shook their heads at the thought of the rash young bridegroom who had dared to play such a trick on the King.

Life was peaceful now in the island kingdom. With his beloved blue cat on his lap, the King forgot how to be angry or cross. Who among his people would be so foolish as to ask questions about the blue cat which had brought this about?

The trick would not have been found out if one night the blue cat had not slipped its head out of the ruby collar. If only it had not jumped out of a low window for a walk on the garden wall! It was not until morning that the cat's absence was noticed. By then it was too late.

Everything was turned upside down in the search for the King's cat. The King himself was sure that bad luck would soon come to the land if the blue cat was not found.

The servants went over the palace, room by room. They looked under the King's bed and behind his throne. But they found no blue cat.

Then someone thought of the garden. And there, in a half-empty laundry tub, they found a strange creature. It was the King's cat, all right, which had fallen into that tub. But, alas, its furry coat was more like a sky dotted with white clouds. The strong soap in the wash water had taken most of the blue dye out of the white fur of the King's former favorite.

You can imagine how angry was that King when he found out how he had been tricked.

"My daughter's husband shall die," he commanded. "Prison is too good for him. He has ruined our kingdom. For it is upon a real blue cat that all our luck depends."

But the Princess loved her young husband. She loved him

very much, and she did not want him to die. So she fell on her knees before her angry father.

"What has he done, Father?" she cried. "You wanted a blue cat. And he made for you a blue cat. You wanted our land to be happy. And this blue cat of his has brought us peace."

"But I wanted the blue cat of my dreams, the cat which the soothsayer swore would bring me good luck." The King would not see reason.

"That blue cat was only a dream, my dear Father." The poor girl now was weeping. "My husband has shown you that a dream is only a dream. Happiness comes if one will only believe in it. You were quite happy when you thought your white cat was a blue cat. Your white cat is truly as good as a blue cat, if you will but think it so."

Just then the pussycat, white now with only a few traces of the blue dye still left, jumped up in its master's lap. The King's anger had been melted by his dear daughter's words. And now he laughed. He rubbed his hands over the blue spots on his pet's coat. And he laughed again.

"Give the cat another bath in that laundry tub," he commanded. "Wash out all this blue foolishness. My daughter is right. A white cat is just as good as a blue cat. From now on there shall be no more dream cats in my kingdom."

*T*HE *MAGIC MANGO*

A King of ancient Annam* once had three fine sons and one
fair daughter. The sons were his pride and joy, but, alas, they
were, all three, taken from him.

The oldest was killed by a tiger in the forest. The second
was drowned in the South China Sea. And the third fell in a
battle with a neighboring king's army.

There was left to this Annamite King only his daughter, the
fair Lotus Blossom. It was bad luck enough to have just a
daughter and no sons at all to say the prayers for their father

* Now a part of Vietnam.

when he at last died. But that this King's only daughter was weak and ill, so weak that she never could leave her bed! Surely she was under the spell of some evil spirit.

It was not that the Princess Lotus Blossom was not beloved. She was as fair as the blossom for which she was named. All who saw her pale face loved her for her sweet smile. And her father, the King, loved her most of all.

From near and far came the doctors that were called in to cure her of her weakness. Even to China across the sea the King sent messengers to bring back medicines that might help her. The Chinese doctors made for her strong powders, ground out of tiger bones. They said she must drink soup made of the livers of dragons. But none of their cures brought color to the pale cheeks of Lotus Blossom. None gave her the strength to rise from her bed.

"There is a witch woman who lives in a cave in the side of the North Mountain," one of his ministers told the King one day. "Everyone says she makes magic. Yesterday she brought back from the dead the wife of a silk merchant. Perhaps she can restore our Princess to health."

The King himself hurried to the cave in the mountainside to find this witch woman. And before he could speak, she knew why he had come.

"I myself cannot cure your daughter, O King. But perhaps the Gods of this Mountain will tell us how to break the spell that keeps her in her bed."

The woman threw a thick gray veil over her head so that no one could see her face. But all in the King's company heard her voice as she talked to the Gods of the Mountain. Then she threw back the veil.

"It can be done," she cried in triumph. "A certain mango can cure the girl. It is a magic mango, and it grows somewhere in this land of Annam. The most perfect of mangoes it is. Smooth, and rosy gold, and as big as a small melon. Its perfume is like flowers."

"But where, Old One, where can this magic mango be found? In whose garden—on what tree does it grow?"

"The Gods did not tell me that." The witch woman shook her head. And the King's face was troubled.

"Let it be known all over our land that the young man who brings the magic mango to my daughter shall have her for his bride." So the King spoke. And his words spread like fire to the farthest ends of his kingdom.

All the youths of Annam searched for the magic mango. Fine youths brought fair fruit to the King's palace. But none of them had the mango which would cure the sick Princess.

Now, on the shores of the South China Sea, there lived a poor fisherman in a little mud hut. Each morning this man and his three sons threw their fishing nets into the ocean. Each night they drew them out again. Sometimes they made a good catch. Sometimes, however, the fish in their nets were few. Like most other fishermen, they had but little money to buy their food and their clothes.

"Our mango tree has good fruit," that fisherman said to his sons when he heard the King's promise. "You, Loo, my oldest son, shall pick the best mangoes and take them to the palace. Heaven grant that the magic mango shall be in one of your baskets. Then you can marry the King's daughter and we shall be rich."

Filled with the mangoes, the baskets on the ends of the carrying pole were heavy on the shoulder of Loo, the fisherman's son. But he was trotting along the path between the rice fields on his way to the palace. Suddenly he met a little old man. His yellow face was wrinkled. His thin beard was gray. One saw at once that this traveler was old enough to be treated with great respect.

"Good day, Good Youth." The little old man gave Loo a friendly greeting. "What are you carrying so fast in your baskets?"

Alas, this oldest son of the fisherman had but little patience with ancient strangers. He had been well taught to be polite to the aged, but he seemed to have forgotten the teaching of his parents.

"Meddlesome old fool," Loo muttered under his breath. "What business is it of yours what I have in my baskets?" Then he spoke aloud, hoping to rid himself of the old man.

"Ai, I have some raw shrimps. I caught them early this morning."

"Let me have a look at your shrimps. Let me lift the green leaves which cover them up."

But Loo rudely pushed the wrinkled old hand away.

"Not for you, Old Man, or for anyone else will I uncover my basket." he cried.

"Well, you say you have shrimps there, my Son, so shrimps you must have." The old man spoke quietly as he turned away. But there was something in his tone of voice which made Loo uneasy.

Finally the fisherman's oldest son reached the King's palace. At first the guards did not wish to let Loo come in. Many young men had already brought mangoes. But none had cured the Princess.

The King had almost lost hope. But he gave the order that this young man should bring his baskets into the room of the

Princess. As she looked on, the green leaves were lifted. But no mangoes were in sight. No, there was only a mass of bad-smelling shrimps. Now Loo knew that the old man had put a spell on his baskets when he had said, "Shrimps you must have."

"This is a bad joke," the angry King cried. The Princess fainted. And the fisherman's oldest son was thrown out of the palace.

At home that night, the young man did not dare tell what had happened. All he said was, "The magic mango was not in my baskets."

"Perhaps Ba, your brother, will have better luck," the fisherman said. And he told his second son to pick the best mangoes that had been left on the glossy green tree. He sent him off with his blessing with two basketsful.

As it happened with Loo, Ba was trotting along with his carrying pole riding upon his shoulder. The baskets of mangoes swung from its ends. Then there came to him the little old man with the wrinkled face and the scanty gray beard.

"Good day, Good Youth," the old man said politely. "What are you carrying so fast in your baskets?"

Now, Ba, the second son of the poor fisherman, like his older brother never minded telling a lie. He, too, would not take the trouble to lift the green leaves and show the mangoes beneath them.

"Old Man, if it is any business of yours, I have a load of elephants' hair. Elephants' hair from Cambodia, which I will sell in the town market." He spoke rudely, as one never should to a man of such a splendid great age.

"Ha!" the old man said then. "Give me a look at your elephants' hair." And he made as if to lift up the leaves.

When Ba pushed his hand away, he continued, "Well, since you say you have elephants' hair, that is what it must be."

The young man did not understand what he meant. He only tossed his foolish head and went along toward the palace.

"More mangoes!" The palace guards were not pleased to see Ba with the baskets swinging from his carrying pole.

"The magic mango had better be there in your baskets," they said as they let him come in. "The King's patience is almost gone. You will feel the rattan rod on your bare back if one of your mangoes does not cure Lotus Blossom."

"Let the baskets be opened." The King gave the order after Ba had saluted him, bowing his head to the ground again and again. "Let the mangoes be seen."

But when the green leaves were lifted, no mangoes were there at all. There was only a tangle of elephants' hair, dirty, bad-smelling, and gray.

It was as the guard had warned Ba. Thirty times the rattan rod fell upon his bare back. He went away home, more dead than alive. He told his fisherman father that a robber band had attacked him. They had beaten him soundly, he said, because he had no money to give them.

"Let me try to find the magic mango, my Father." It was Nop, the third son of this fisherman on the South China Sea. "Perhaps good luck will be mine. Perhaps one of the mangoes I take will make Princess Lotus Blossom strong again. Then she will be my bride."

Nop's brothers laughed. His father looked doubtful. This youngest of his three sons was more gentle than his older brothers. They often called him a sissy because he was polite to every person he met. Young Nop was known on that seashore as a youth who had never in his life told a lie.

"There are only a few mangoes left on our tree," his father objected. "They are the smallest and the poorest. And they are high in the treetop."

"I would climb even up to the sky to reach the magic mango if it will cure the King's daughter." Nop was determined.

"Go then," said his father. "But watch out for those robbers who treated your brother so badly."

"When I marry the Princess, we shall be rich." The good youth was already dreaming of his share in the King's treasures. "I will build for you a stone house. You shall have a water buffalo to plow the land behind our house. There shall be pigs and chickens in our courtyard and ducks on the lake."

With these fine promises, Nop went trotting along the path between the rice fields. His baskets of mangoes danced as he ran. But he did not feel the weight of the carrying pole. He was so happy at the thought that if the Gods wished, he would marry the Princess.

"What do you carry in your baskets, my Son?" It was the same little old man with the wrinkled face and gray beard. And it was the same question he had asked of Nop's brothers, Loo and Ba.

But the old man did not receive the same kind of answer this time. Nop did not think up a lie or brush the old man aside.

"Mangoes I have, Honorable Old One," he replied politely. "My mangoes are juicy and fresh, although they are not very big. Somehow I am sure that among them is the magic mango which will cure the King's daughter. Pray for me, Old One, that that magic mango may be among them."

"Mangoes you say they are, and indeed mangoes they are." The old man had lifted the green leaves and was gazing upon the fruit. "And the magic mango, indeed, may well be among them."

It was many hours before the palace guards would let this third son of the fisherman inside the palace. It was more hours before the King would receive him and take him and his mangoes to the Princess.

But at last the green leaves were lifted. And the King and his daughter looked down at the finest mangoes that had ever been seen in that land.

Nop's eyes were round with wonder. For the fruit he had picked from the top of the mango tree had been only the size of plums. Now every one was as big as a small melon. Their flowery perfume filled the room where the Princess lay on her couch. The smooth round sides of the mangoes gleamed like the golden crown of a King.

"At last, here we have mangoes fit for Lotus Blossom to eat. Try one, my Daughter. And Heaven send that it be the magic mango which will cure you."

Shouts of joy rang through the palace. For Lotus Blossom, with her first bite of Nop's mango, had risen from her bed. Her pale face was now as rosy as the sunrise. Quickly she walked out onto her balcony, where all the people could see her. She was quite well and strong again.

The King ordered that the wedding feast be held the next day. A gown of bright silk was brought for Nop, and satin shoes were put on his feet. No one would have known that Nop was a poor fisherman's son. In his fine clothes, and with the goodness that shone out of his eyes, he was a fit bridegroom for any king's daughter.

For three days the people ate, danced, and sang. Everyone

made merry, and for ever after the fair Lotus Blossom lived happily with her good husband.

Nop did not forget the words he had spoken when he left his old home. A new stone house was built on the spot where the fisherman's mud hut had stood. Pigs rooted, and chickens scratched in the courtyard. The water buffalo was bought, and ducks swam on the pond. So Nop was able to keep his promise, all because of his politeness to the little old man.

THE ELEPHANT'S LIP

Have you ever really looked at an elephant's lip?

Have you noticed how sadly it droops there under the beast's long gray trunk?

Perhaps you think that this drooping lip was an accident. Or that the Maker-of-All-Things meant it to be like that.

Well, that's not the way people thought of it long ago in Laos, that South Asian country just next to Thailand.

There are many elephants in Laos. Every man, woman, and child in that land can see for himself just how such a beast looks. They all know that an elephant's lower lip droops sadly, like a piece of gray cloth.

"The elephant's lip was not shaped like that in the beginning." So the Laos grandmothers used to tell their grandchildren in other times. "The huge creature's ears were just the same, floppy and wide. Its trunk was just as long and just as strong. But its lip was quite different. It was a gay, happy lip that looked as though the creature was always smiling."

Then the Laos grandmothers would go on to tell what happened to change the shape of the elephant's lip. This is their story.

In the long-ago times, there was a poor man and his wife who lived in a jungle hut in the backcountry. Twelve children they had, and every one was a girl.

How should a poor man find food enough for so many daughters? A girl cannot hunt. A girl cannot help her father cut down teak trees in the forest. Girls were really of little use in such a part of the country.

There was never quite enough rice in that jungle hut. Not even enough to feed the man and his wife. So at last one day he said, "Wife, I am growing old. I can no longer work to get food enough for our twelve hungry daughters. They are young. They are strong. Let them go out and find their own food for themselves."

His wife wept many tears. She loved her daughters well. But no doubt her husband was right. Someone would care for the girls, surely. So she helped get ready a basket, which the man set down before his twelve daughters.

It seemed to be a big basket of rice. That is what the twelve girls thought it was when they helped their father carry it into the jungle. They were told he was taking them on a hunting trip to look for rabbits for their supper.

He led the twelve girls deep, deep into the forest. This way
and that way they went, twisting and turning, until they were
quite lost. He wanted to make sure they would never find
their way home again.

"You shall cook this rice for your dinner over our campfire," the father said. "I shall go look for the rabbits. When I
have killed enough, I will call you to help me to skin them and
take them home."

Of course he never came back. And it was not long before
the twelve sisters found out he had left them there, deep in
the jungle, to look out for themselves. For, as soon as they
dipped into their food basket, they saw there was only a thin
layer of rice on the top. Underneath this, alas, the basket was
filled with gray ashes from old cooking fires.

"Ai! Ai!" they wept. "Our father has left us in this jungle
to starve." And they clung to each other.

When the dark came, the twelve slept close together upon
the jungle path. The beasts of the forest found them there,
but no wild creature harmed them. Not even the fierce tiger
whose breath fanned their faces when he sniffed at their hair.

Next day when the sun opened the skies, they rose from
their hard bed on the ground. They bathed in a stream and
then began to look about them for some wild fruit or berries.
They were busy searching the bushes when they spied an old
woman. She gave them a friendly smile as she came toward
them.

"What do you do here, so far from home, dear young
people?" She spoke in a kind tone.

"Ai! Ai!" The girls wept as they told her their sad story. How
their father had left them in the deep forest to find food for
themselves! And how hungry they were!

"There is rice in my cooking pot," the old woman said. "You shall come home with me. You shall live under my roof of thatch. I shall be glad of your company." With a beckoning finger, she led the way down the jungle path.

Now these twelve sisters knew that they should not trust strangers. But this woman seemed kind. And, indeed, they were hungry. So they gladly went with her to a little clearing in the midst of the woods. A broad roof of thatch was there, held up on four posts. It gave shelter for all twelve of them and the woman as well. Best of all was the pot of rice bubbling over the cooking fire.

"I must go back into the jungle," the old woman said when they had finished their meal. "Rest here in my home until I return. You may swim in the river. You may pick my mangoes if you like. But you must never—no, never—go down that little path." She pointed to a single track which led through a thicket. And she shook her finger fiercely so that they should remember her words.

As soon as the old woman had gone, the sisters looked at one another. There was fear in their eyes.

"What is there down that little path which we must not see?" This was the question they asked one another.

"We must find out right away, Sisters. I will go first," the oldest of the twelve said at last.

Their bare brown feet made no noise at all as they ran down the forbidden path.

"Ai! Ai!" cried their leader when the path led into a small open space amid the trees.

"Ai! Ai!" cried the others. "Here are the bare bones of people, people who once were alive as we are!" Their eyes were wide with horror as they looked at the many bones piled up there on the ground.

"The old woman eats people. That is quite clear. She will cook us and eat us, too, if we do not run away." The sisters had heard stories of cannibal witches who lured people into their homes.

"The old woman is such a witch," the oldest girl cried. "Come, let us run."

The sisters ran and they ran, as fast as ever they could, away from that witch woman's thatched hut in the forest.

"I hear someone running after us," the last girl called out to the others. "The witch woman is coming. Oh, what shall we do?"

As her words were spoken, a giant buffalo cow came to drink in the stream by the side of their path.

"Help us, Cow, help us!" the sisters cried out. "Hide us from the witch woman who eats people."

Strange things seem to have happened in those ancient times. But none was more strange than what took place then on the banks of that jungle stream.

That buffalo cow opened her mouth. Wider and wider she stretched it. So great was her throat that the twelve girls jumped right into it, one after the other. Somehow or other they found room to hide themselves inside the animal's stomach.

Please do not ask how this could be. I do not know either. I only know that's how the tale was told long ago.

When the witch woman found the water buffalo cow, there was no sign of the sisters.

"Have you seen my twelve daughters, Cow? Which way did they go?" the witch woman cried.

"No daughters of yours are here," the cow replied. And, of course, that was the truth, for the girls were not daughters of the old witch.

But the old woman flew into a rage. "They were here. I followed their footprints. Tell me which way they went or I'll make an end of you." She was terrible in her anger.

"Ah! Well, yes, they were here," the cow replied quietly. "But they ran off that way. They were running like the wind. If you want to catch them, you must run that way fast too."

The cow tossed her horns to point out the way. And the old woman flew off again, running and running.

"Out you come now, and quickly, for the old hag may turn round," the cow called to the girls. She opened her mouth wide, wide, and again wider. And out jumped the twelve. They thanked the good cow who had hidden them so well. Then they darted off in the opposite direction through the deep woods.

"I hear someone running." The warning came again from the last girl in the procession. "The witch woman has found our footprints again. She is coming our way."

Just then there came, crashing out of the woods, a great cow elephant. She was a big beast, bigger by far than anyone sees today.

"Hide us, Good Elephant, Queen of the Jungle!" the twelve girls cried out as if with one voice. "The witch woman is coming. She will strip our bones bare."

"Quick, then. Be quick, my Daughters! Jump into my mouth!" The great beast dropped down on her knees. She raised her long trunk. Higher and higher she raised it. Wider and wider she opened her mouth and stretched her soft, smiling lower lip. "Be quick, for I hear the woman. She is very near."

Somehow the girls did not move quite quickly enough. The youngest was slow to get herself inside the elephant's open mouth. Her gray dress was not all pulled in after her when the old woman appeared.

"Give me my twelve daughters, Elephant," the witch demanded.

"No daughters of yours are here." The elephant knew well that the sisters did not belong to the cannibal woman. She lifted her trunk as she shouted the words.

"Then what is that bit of a girl's dress hanging out of your mouth, Beast?" The woman pointed to a bit of gray cloth which still could be seen. The youngest girl had not been at all clever in hiding herself in the elephant's throat.

"That is my own lip, Woman." The elephant stamped her great feet. She towered high above the witch, who fairly danced in her anger at losing her prizes.

The old woman ground her teeth. She, too, stamped her feet. Her magic was strong. But it was not strong enough to harm a creature so powerful as this biggest of all the beasts.

"You say that bit of gray cloth is your own lip?" she screamed. "Well, your own lip it always shall be. I put a spell on your mouth. For ever and ever your lip shall hang down like the end of the girl's dress."

There was nothing for her to do but go away without the twelve sisters, who were protected by the cow elephant. How they got along after that I do not know. But for then they were safe. No doubt they met other strangers who were kinder than the witch woman would have been.

The next time you come across an elephant, take a good look at its lower lip. Then you can decide for yourself whether the spell of the witch woman worked.

THE SHIPWRECKED PRINCE

The three sons of a certain King in India were not at all alike. The two older ones were good young Princes, always at hand to do their father's bidding. The third one, the youngest, whose name was Hatan, was good at heart, too. But he liked excitement and adventure.

Hatan loved to ride and to hunt. None in that kingdom could tame a wild horse or kill a fierce beast better than he.

His father, however, feared that this youngest son, like the horses he rode and the beasts he shot in the game forest, was becoming too wild. He was too often away from his studies with the palace tutors.

"You must settle down, Hatan," he told the young Prince one day. "You must pay more attention to learning about the affairs of our kingdom. It takes more than riding and hunting to fit a prince for ruling a country like ours. Never, I think, will I dare to make you heir to this throne. You will not make a good king."

Now, Prince Hatan was proud. His father's words hurt him. In his own heart he was sure he could rule a land wisely and well.

"Since I can never be a king here," he told his father, "I will go forth and find a kingdom somewhere else. Give me your blessing, my Father, and I will sail across the wide waters. I will travel to the farthest ends of the earth, until I come to a land which will have me for its king."

"Foolish Hatan!" the King sighed. "You are too proud and too bold. Who will look after you at the ends of the earth, as we have cared for you here?" At first the King would not hear of his youngest son's plan. But the young man gave him no peace.

"Set me aboard a ship. Let me sail away over the sea. And when you see me again, I promise you I shall have a golden throne as fine as your own." How could the young Prince know that just such good fortune was in store for him?

At last Hatan won his father's consent. The ship's sails were spread. And the winds carried the ship far out upon the great sea. All was going well on that ship until the storm came. Then dark clouds blackened the sky. The winds grew stronger and stronger. Rain fell in torrents. Waves dashed high, high, up over the vessel.

Up and down! The ship pitched like a leaf, tossed by strong winds. From one side to another it rolled, in the deep troughs of the ocean. At last one giant wave picked up Hatan's ship and broke it into two pieces as if it were a dry twig.

Into the water went all on that ship. Only young Hatan was saved from the stormy sea. A strong board, torn out of the ship's side, floated within his reach, and he took a firm hold of it. So great was the young man's strength that the angry waves were not able to tear the board from him. And he floated safely upon it for many days.

Then, one fine morning, the ocean was calm again. And the waves gently washed the Prince and his board up onto a sunny shore.

Never had Hatan seen such a fair land. Its green gardens were filled with flowers of every color. In its orchards were trees bearing fruit, ripe for the eating. It was truly a paradise. And not far from the seashore, the Prince saw the shining white towers of a magnificent city.

"A land like this I shall rule one day." Hatan spoke aloud. Again who knows what put such magic words into his mouth?

To the gate of the King's palace the shipwrecked Prince made his way. His clothes had been torn to rags by the stormy waves. At first the palace guards took him for a beggar and were about to turn him away.

But the King's gardener happened to be there, and he was a man with a kind heart. He stopped to hear the story which the shipwrecked young Prince was telling the guards.

"My ship sank beneath me. But a miracle saved me from going down with it, as my shipmates did. I am cast up on these shores without shelter or food and in these old rags. If I may but come in, I will repay your kindness in any way you may wish."

The young man spoke politely. Even in such ragged clothing, it was clear that he was no ordinary beggar. The King's gardener took pity upon him.

"I will give you clothing and food, my good young man," that kind-hearted man said. "You shall sleep under the roof of my gardener's house. And in return you shall help me with the King's flowers and fruit trees."

Hatan learned quickly to tend the King's garden. He liked best of all to cut the fresh flowers which were carried each day into the palace.

One morning when the gardener himself had been called away, it fell to the Prince to take the bright blossoms into the King's council chamber. He himself put the brilliant blooms into their vases of silver and gold. Such beauty did he give the room that the King was delighted.

"Summon the gardener," the King cried. And when the man came, he made him a gift of several pieces of gold. "Let the flowers, always hereafter, be arranged in this manner," he said to the surprised man, who had returned to the palace from his errand outside.

Perhaps the gardener should have then told the truth to the King—that it was his new helper, and not himself, who had arranged the flowers that day. But he did not. He was only careful, from then on, that it should be Hatan who should do this work.

It was while Hatan was busy with his flowers inside the palace one morning that he was seen by the King's youngest daughter.

"Who are you?" she demanded. "Why have I never seen you before?" This was a noble and handsome young man. And the girl listened to the story of his sea journey and shipwreck with wondering eyes. She believed him when he said he was the son of a distant King.

Each morning she waited for Hatan to bring the blossoms into the palace. Day after day she made him tell her about his

father's kingdom. And it was not very long before the two young people were deeply in love.

When the Princess told her father she had found the one she wanted to marry, the King was troubled.

"It is true that this young man is an artist in arranging our flowers," he said. "But a gardener's helper is not a fit husband for the daughter of a King." The courtiers nodded their heads. Truly a servant was not the bridegroom they would choose for their princess.

"My loved one is no servant." The Princess read their minds. "He is a noble Prince, the son of an East Indian king. And if I cannot marry him, I will not marry at all."

The King loved his daughter. He, too, had been struck with the noble look of Hatan. He wanted to believe the story of the distant kingdom from which the Prince's ship had sailed. And so he gave his consent.

The marriage took place. There was feasting and dancing that lasted a month, and a palace was provided for the young couple. Fine clothes and jewels were given them, and everyone rejoiced.

Everyone, that is, except the husbands of the three other daughters of the King. They were jealous of this newcomer. They often declared that the story of his being a prince was only a lie.

"Hatan has surely bewitched our father-in-law," they said among themselves. "He has made himself the King's favorite by some underhand trick. Everywhere the King goes, this upstart goes with him. We must do something about it before it is too late."

"Yes, we must prove to the King that this stranger from over the sea is no prince but a servant, as we have always declared."

They all agreed to this, but how to do it was another matter.

"Let us challenge Hatan to go hunting. He has never mounted a horse since he came to this land. No doubt he cannot ride. Nor can he throw a spear. A hunt will prove to the King that his fourth daughter's husband has had no noble training at all."

This was their plot. When they suggested a hunt, Prince Hatan agreed at once. He examined the hunting spear and the knife they gave to him. But, to their surprise, he did not go to the stables to make sure he was to be given a safe horse.

"You see, we are right." The three plotters were happy. "Hatan is afraid to go near the horses. We shall arrange it so that the only steed left for him to ride shall be the wild stallion which no one can mount."

The morning of the hunt came. With the dawn, Hatan rose and went off to find his horse. At the stables there was only one horse, the wild stallion, tossing its head and rolling its eyes.

The stablemen could not believe their eyes when they saw the young Prince leap onto the back of the plunging horse. The stallion reared. Then it bucked. It whirled round and round. Then it was off, like a bolt of lightning, into the game forest.

"Aha! This is like being at home again," Hatan shouted in glee. And the stallion soon found that this rider had no fear. It was not long before it was cantering quietly down the trail through the trees.

In no time at all, the Prince's spear had brought down a leopard, a jackal, and a bear. Of course, Hatan could not carry these large animals on the back of the wild stallion. Instead, with his hunting knife, the young man cut off the tail of the jackal, an ear of the leopard, and the nose tip of the bear.

These he wrapped in a silk handkerchief so that he could take them with him to his home.

"Why have you come back so soon?" The King's daughter came running to meet her young husband. She was troubled to see him returning from the stables before the other hunters had started.

"Oh, I have finished my part of the hunt," he explained. "I have killed a leopard, a bear, and a jackal, and that should be enough for one day." Then he showed her the bear's nose, the leopard's ear, and the jackal's tail.

"Put these in a safe place, dear Wife," he said. "It may well be I shall need them."

The sun was high overhead when the three plotters mounted their horses. When they saw the wild stallion in his part of the stable, they did not guess it had already been ridden that morning.

"We are right," they said again. "The King's favorite is a coward who does not know how to hunt. He is afraid of the wild horse." And they rode gaily out to try their own skill in the game forest.

But fortune did not smile on these three that day. No wild animals could they find, no matter which way they rode. And not one beast did they kill.

"We cannot go back empty-handed," they cried. And when they came upon the dead bear and the leopard and the jackal, they decided to claim them for themselves. They had their servants bring them in, saying that they had killed them.

The King had set a time to receive his four sons-in-law to hear of their luck in the game forest.

"What beasts have you killed?" he asked when they stood before him.

"A bear, a jackal, and a leopard we have killed, O King." This was the lie which the three plotters told. "We have had our servants bring in the dead animals for you to see. They are at the palace gate." The three felt quite safe, you see. They truly believed their other brother-in-law had not left his palace that morning.

"And you, Hatan, my son?" The King turned toward his favorite. But before Hatan could answer, the three spoke for him.

"O King, it is as we said: this one is no noble prince but a poor coward."

"We did not see him in the game forest."

"He has not left his palace this day."

There was silence then. Everyone waited to hear what Hatan would say.

"A leopard, a jackal, and a bear have been killed, O King," the young man began. "That much is true. But it was I who killed the three beasts, not these lying three. On the wild stallion I rode forth at the dawn. And it was my spear which brought to earth these three animals which lie at the palace gate."

"Not only is Hatan a coward but he tells lies," the other sons-in-law shouted. "He cannot prove that it was he who killed the beasts." The three plotters were beginning to be afraid. They must try their best to keep the King from finding out that they had lied.

"Ask the stablemen if our brother-in-law truly rode the wild stallion," they demanded, so sure were they that the Prince had not ridden out of the palace that day.

So the stablemen were called before the King.

"Indeed, the young Prince did ride the wild stallion," the

stablemen cried. "At the break of day it was. And such riding has never before been seen in this land. Like the lightning, the stallion took him into the game forest. Like the wind, he came back again before any of the other hunters was awake. And that wild horse was as quiet as a lamb when Prince Hatan put him back into the stable."

This was indeed a wonder to hear. And the King was about to say so, when one of the three plotters spoke again.

"That does not prove it was Hatan who killed the beasts." He was fighting to save himself and his two companions in the plot.

"That can be proved, however," Hatan declared. "Send a servant to my palace. Let him bring back from my wife the three things which I gave her to keep for me when I came back from the hunt."

The whispering among the courtiers grew louder. What three things could there be that would prove Hatan the winner of this hunting contest?

When the silken kerchief was opened, there were shouts of surprise. For there lay the bear's nose, the leopard's ear, and the tail of the jackal.

Then Hatan spoke: "Here is proof, O King. Proof that I killed the three beasts. I could not carry their bodies upon the wild stallion. So I cut off the tip of the bear's nose, an ear of the leopard, and the jackal's tail. If you will examine the dead animals at the palace gate, you will see that the bear is without a nose, the leopard is without one ear, and the jackal has no tail."

And, of course, that is how it was.

The King was delighted to find his favorite the winner. No

one disagreed when he said that Prince Hatan should rule the land after his death.

What about the three liars? Well, Prince Hatan, like the King's gardener, had a good heart. At his own request, they were not punished, as perhaps they should have been. And this noble action completely won their affection for the King's heir.

As we all know, everyone has to die someday. And at last death came to that King. Young Prince Hatan was crowned and given his place on the throne. There was a fine ceremony, and the most honored of all the guests from afar was the father of the shipwrecked Prince.

It was as Hatan had foretold. Now, when his father found him again, he had his own golden throne and he ruled over a fair land.

THE TAILOR'S BRIGHT DAUGHTER

Long ago, when the country of Iraq was known as Arabia, there was a young Caliph who was handsome and greatly loved by his people. It was a fine sight to see him ride forth from his palace on his way to the hunt. Silver shone on the saddle of his white riding camel. Gold thread gleamed in his garments. Everyone bowed low when this Caliph rode through the streets of his city.

One morning, however, there was a man in the watching crowds who did not bow. Instead of bending low before the great man, this fellow stood up, straight and tall. And, in a loud voice, he cried out for all to hear: "Look well at our Caliph! See his fine jacket of gold cloth! Note his flowing red cape! It is I who made these glorious garments for the Son of Heaven. I, Abou Adi, tailor to the Caliph, made them in my shop in the Street of the Cape Makers."

The Caliph heard the man's boasting and he laughed aloud. He shook his head, and he thought, "Our tailor is too proud. Someone should teach him a lesson."

The young Caliph did not halt his white camel that day to speak to the bold tailor. But he did not forget. The very next time he walked out on the city streets, he came upon the proud man. They met on the highway which led to the edge of the city, and the Caliph fell into step with him.

"Let us walk a little together, Abou Adi." The Caliph spoke in a warm, friendly voice.

Then, truly, that tailor swelled with importance. His face grew red with pleasure. It seemed as if he would burst with his pride in being the Caliph's companion.

"The cape I am wearing today is one which you made for me, Abou Adi," the Caliph began. "It is a good cape and well made, but the camel's-wool cloth is not of the best."

"Yet, as Your Honor has said, it is a good garment." This tailor could scarcely bear to hear any but words of praise for his capes. "Truly a good cape depends chiefly upon the way it is made, Sire. I can make a good cape out of any material, any material at all. And everyone will say, 'That is a good garment.'"

The Caliph smiled. Here was the chance he was seeking to teach the proud fellow a lesson.

"Did you say any material at all, Abou Adi? Can you truly make a good cape, no matter what material you use?"

"Indeed, of any material, O Caliph." The tailor was puzzled by this curious question.

"That you shall prove, Abou Adi." The Caliph's voice suddenly was cold and stern. He looked round about them. And his eyes fell on a large red rock at the side of the highway.

"That red stone over there, Tailor!" He pointed. "It has a bright, pleasing color. Take that stone home with you and make me a cape. Be sure that it shall be a good cape."

"A cape made of stone, O Caliph? Who ever heard of a cape

made of stone?" The tailor's voice now was no longer boastful and sure.

"Make good your own words, Abou Adi. You boasted that you could make a good cape of any material. That you shall do. Or you shall be put to death."

The poor tailor believed that the Caliph was in earnest. And he was afraid.

"Woe! Woe!" he cried to his wife and his daughter that evening. "How can anyone make a cape out of stone? I am as good as dead now."

He wept. His wife wept. But Nira, his young daughter, spoke comforting words to him. She was the prettiest girl in all the Caliph's great city. She was the brightest one, too. So clever was she that her father always listened well to what she had to say.

"You shall catch the Caliph in this trap he has set for you, my Father," she cried. "You shall make his command into the joke which it really is. The Caliph will be amused. And his trap for you will be forgotten."

Then she explained to Abou Adi just what he should do.

Next morning the Caliph was surprised to see the tailor come into his court. The man was bowing and smiling. And he was dragging behind him a large leather bag.

"Honorable Caliph," Abou Adi began, "when I reached home last evening, at once I went to work to obey your command. Your stone cape is cut. It is ready for sewing. But, as you well know, a tailor cannot sew without thread. The only proper thread for a cape of stone would be thread spun out of sand. So I have brought here, in this bag, the right kind of sand. When your spinners have spun it into thread, I will finish your cape."

The Caliph laughed. He knew well that his command was impossible to fulfill, and he had truly meant it for a joke. So he laughed loud and long at the clever trick which the tailor was using to escape from the trap he had set for him.

"Who thought of asking for thread spun out of sand, Abou Adi?" the Caliph asked. "Surely it was not you yourself. Your wits are more in your needle."

The tailor hung his head. Then he laughed too.

"You are right, Sire. It was not I but my daughter, young Nira. She is as bright as she is pretty."

"A pretty girl who is as clever as Nira must be fit to be wife to a Caliph. I shall take her for my bride."

Now, in those days in that ancient land of Arabia, a Caliph could have as many wives as he liked. This young ruler already had ever so many. Perhaps that is why, once the wedding was over, he completely forgot he had married the tailor's bright daughter. Indeed, after the ceremony, he did not even take time to lift up her veil and look upon her fair face. He only gave orders that she should have a palace of her own, fine clothes, and servants to wait upon her.

Once in a long time, the Caliph remembered her. When he rode past her palace, he would call out, "Hello! Hello, Tailor's Daughter! Peace be with you."

The girl would have time only to call back, "Allah send you peace," before the Caliph was gone, riding swiftly to his hunting out on the desert. She never had a chance to come forth so that he should see what a pretty girl he had wed.

People thought Nira was lucky there in her fine palace. She had servants to do her bidding. She had rich food to eat and silken robes to wear. But, instead, her heart was sad. She had fallen in love with the Caliph, and she wanted to be his true wife.

"Think, my Daughter, think hard!" the tailor said when Nira told him she was lonely. "You who have wits as sharp as my needles should be able to find some way to reach your husband's heart."

"If the Caliph would only take time to look at me and talk to me a little, perhaps I could make him love me," the girl replied. "No doubt he thinks the daughter of a mere tailor is not a fit companion for a caliph."

When she was by herself, Nira thought, "I must go out to find my husband since he will not come to me here. I must meet him without telling him who I really am."

The next time the young ruler rode out into the desert to hunt the gazelles he pitched his camp far away on the very edge of his country. And it was to that place that Nira, the tailor's bright daughter, came with her camel train and her tent.

It was in the cool of the evening. A roast kid had been eaten. And the Caliph was lolling on the sandy floor of his tent. He was leaning comfortably back against his camel saddle of leather, and a servant was passing him a small brass cup filled with coffee.

The Caliph took his first sip. He made a wry face and he spat out the drink.

"Do you try to poison me, Fellow?" he angrily cried to the servant. "You have put salt in my coffee. You shall suffer for this."

The coffee maker fell at his master's feet. "Forgive me, Lord Caliph," he begged. "It is the fault of the girl in the strange silken tent which stands near our camp. Her beauty has bewitched me. I did not know that I put salt into your cup."

"What girl in what tent? Speak, Man, what is this riddle?"

"There is a tent of heavy silk, fit for a queen, Master. And its owner walks before it, without mantle or veil to cover her face. Her beauty shines like the moon. Her eyes are bright as two jewels. Her robe is that of a Princess. Is it beyond understanding, sire, that I so lost my senses as to mistake salt for sugar."

The man's words roused the curiosity of the young Caliph.

"Let the girl be brought to me here," he commanded. "I shall see for myself whether you are speaking the truth."

Well, the Caliph was as much taken with Nira's fair face as the coffee maker had been. Indeed, he fell in love with her at first sight. And, after the manner of Caliphs, who take what they will, he took her for his wife, out there on the desert.

Why did not Nira tell the Caliph who she was? Perhaps she still thought he would look down on her if he knew she was only a tailor's daughter. No doubt she believed she could hold his interest longer if she was a mystery to him.

There in the desert she found her heart's desire. She became the Caliph's true wife.

For three days and three nights they feasted together. She sang him sweet songs. She made him laugh with her bright sayings. The Caliph was charmed with his new bride. He loved her so much that he was not even disturbed when she beat him in games of chess. Instead he gave her as the winner's prize his own golden ring.

On the morning of the fourth day, the day set for the Caliph's return to the city, Nira's silken tent was already gone. His desert bride had disappeared in the night, as if she had been carried away by the wind.

The Caliph and his camel riders searched all that part of the desert. But no trace of her could they find.

Sadly the Caliph mounted his white camel and rode back to his palace. Who was his fair desert bride? Where could he find her again? He asked here. He asked there. No one knew the answer.

Why did not Nira send a message to her dear husband? Perhaps she meant to tell him when he rode past her palace. Each time he called out "hello," she ran to the door. But, as before, he was gone when she tried to show him her face.

"He would not believe that his desert bride was only the tailor's daughter," she said to herself. "He would not believe, either, that a baby son has been born to us."

It is hard to understand—and the story does not explain—why seven full years went by without the Caliph's finding this one of his brides whom he loved the best.

Twice again Nira had visited the Caliph in his camps on the desert. And twice she had lost courage to tell him the truth. Two more sons had been born to them, one each time after she had returned again to her palace. And during each of her visits, the Caliph had given her as a present something which belonged to him. One was a jeweled dagger. The other was a silk headcloth.

Then one day came the news that the Caliph was to marry a princess from a neighboring land. None of his many wives had given him a son to rule the land after his death. Perhaps this new bride would be more blessed by Heaven, the Caliph said.

Nira was frightened now. She feared that the chosen Princess would take her place in the heart of the young Caliph. And she thought what she must do.

The wedding day came. Crowds gathered at the gate of the

palace to see the bride arrive. And in the very front of the throng at the very gate itself stood three fine little boys. The oldest one, who was about six years old, held the two younger ones by the hand.

The Caliph came out to greet his foreign bride, and at once the oldest child stepped into his path. His mother Nira had schooled him well.

"I have gifts for you on your wedding day, O Caliph." The child spoke in a clear voice. And he put into the Caliph's hand his royal ring, his jeweled dagger, and his silken headcloth.

"But these are the gifts I presented to my dear bride of the desert?" The Caliph's voice was filled with wonder. "Who are you, Boy?"

"I am your son, O my Father; and these other two also are your own children. Nira, the daughter of Abou Adi, your tailor, is our mother. She followed her lord out into the desert. And she pitched her tent near your camp. There she became your wife for a second, a third, and a fourth time." The boy had learned his piece well.

"Allah be praised! At last I have found my dear one." The young Caliph lost no time in making his way to Nira's palace. This time she was standing to receive him outside her door.

One must feel sorry, perhaps, for the Princess of the neighboring kingdom, who was left at the gate of the Caliph's own palace. For, of course, she was sent back to her own land. Rich presents may have helped her in her disappointment. But, however that was, from then on Nira sat by the side of the young Caliph in his council room. With her bright wits she was able to help him rule his people well.

FIRE MAGIC AND THE MUD HEN

Once, men did not know the magic secret of making fire. At least that is what people used to say in Pacific Islands on the other side of the world.

Of course, they knew about fire itself. They knew about the Great Fire which came out of their volcanoes. No one can remember now when there were not these fiery mountains on the Islands of the Pacific Ocean.

The Islanders knew, too, how to use the heat of the red-hot lava which sometimes rolled down the sides of the volcanoes. They found it good to cook their fish and their sweet potatoes. Foods such as these tasted better when they were cooked.

But they did not know how to make the fire magic themselves. This was before they found out the secret of making fire from the little mud hen.

Since the Islanders did not know how to make just a small fire, they often had to eat their fish raw. They could not boil their taro roots. Nor could they roast their sweet potatoes.

But, strangely, now and then, an Islander would come upon a small fire just before it died out.

"Today I saw the place where a small fire had been," that Islander would tell his friends. "There was a potato left in its ashes, and it was still warm."

"Why did you not bring home the small fire?" the others would ask. They badly wanted to find out the secret of this useful means of cooking their food.

"There was no red fire left in those ashes." This was the usual answer. "The red fire had gone. The black sticks were still warm. But they would not make more fire."

No one could find out who had made these small fires. So the chief of that island called his people about him.

"We must find the magic secret of making the small fire," he said. "There shall be a rich reward for that one who makes the discovery."

All the young men of the island said they would try. But none was so eager as a boy whose name was Kokoa.

"I shall find the fire magic," Kokoa said to his old grand-mother the next day. He was a bold youth, as you can guess from these words. He was bolder, as it turned out, than his three older brothers. For they quickly grew tired of looking for fires. Soon they went back to their fishing out on the sea.

Now, the grandmother of Kokoa was a very old woman. She was a very wise woman, too. Indeed, she knew secrets that were hidden from other people. Some even said she was a witch. And it was she who helped her young grandson when he set forth to look for the small fire.

"It is the mud hens you must watch, Kokoa," she said. "It is the mud hens who alone know the secret of making fire."

Kokoa knew he would find the mud hens in the wet, marshy

parts of the island. Once he had caught a mud hen. He had seen its short wings and its short tail. He had looked well at its long toes, on which it could run so well in the mud. He knew he could pick out the mud hens from among all other birds.

"Yes, it is the mud hens who know about the small fires," Kokoa's grandmother told him. "They cook the fish they pick out of the chief's fishpond. They cook the sweet potatoes they steal from our garden patch. I have seen them with my own eyes.

"Hide near the chief's fishpond, Kokoa. But do not let the mud hens catch sight of you. If they do not know you are near, you may perhaps watch them call forth the small fire."

His three brothers went with Kokoa as far as the chief's fishpond. But there they left him. They went out on the sea in their fishing boat.

Kokoa looked at the shallow pond with the marshy banks all around it. He could see the chief's potato patch and his plantings of taro roots. Here there was fish in plenty. Here he was sure to meet up with the mud hens.

The boy hid in the tall reeds that grew around the edge of the pond. He squatted down low so that his head would not show above their waving tops. And he waited for the mud hens to come for their fish and make their fire.

It was not long before there was the sound of birds running through the grass. There was the chirping of the mud hens as they came out on the edge of the chief's fishpond.

"Some are digging potatoes," Kokoa said to himself. "Some are taking fish from the water. There are others gathering sticks." The boy held his breath. Perhaps, indeed, he would see them make fire.

But one of the birds—perhaps the oldest and wisest—called out to the others.

"Wait!" the old bird warned them. "Four boys were here just now. We must see if they are still near." And he flew up to the top of a tall coconut palm tree. He looked out at the sea to find the small boat with Kokoa's three brothers in it.

"One! Two! Three!" the bird counted. "But there were four. Where is the other one? He may be watching us. Do not make a fire!"

The mud hens threw down the dry sticks they had gathered. They dropped their fish and potatoes. And they flew away, scolding in their high, chirping voices.

"The mud hens were too clever, Grandmother," Kokoa said that night when he went home. "They somehow knew I was watching them."

"Mud hens are wise birds, Kokoa, or they would not know the secret of making fire." The old woman nodded her head. "But we can outwit them. Tomorrow you must make a bundle of rags. Tie them together so they will look like a boy. Put the rag boy with your three brothers when they go out in their boat. The mud hens will think it is you."

Next day the boys set the rag figure in the center of their small boat. A paddle was laid beside it. At a distance no one, not even a clever old bird, could tell that this dummy was not a boy.

All went as before. Kokoa hid in the rushes beside the chief's fishpond. The mud hens came running out of the marsh. Some caught fish or dug up the chief's sweet potatoes. Others picked up sticks for the fire.

Kokoa could not see very well through the reeds. He did not dare raise his head high.

"The mud hens used dry sticks to call forth their small fire," the boy told his grandmother that night. "I saw the smoke and the red fire. I smelled their fish and potatoes. But they put out the red fire when they went away. Alas, I did not find out their secret."

"You will have to catch one of the mud hens in your own hands. Then you can force it to tell you the secret," his grandmother told Kokoa that night. "Wait until they are busy with their cooking. They will turn their potatoes over and over with their beaks to be sure they are done on both sides. So they will not see you. But you will need to be quick."

Kokoa remembered his grandmother's words the next day. He surprised the busy birds. And in the scramble he caught one of the mud hens by the leg.

"Squawk! Sque-e-e-k!" The little mud hen cried out to her sisters to come to her rescue.

But they all ran away into the reeds. The only answer she had was, "Don't tell! Don't you dare tell! Don't show him how to make the small fire. Or we will kill you."

"But you shall tell!" Kokoa cried. His fingers were tight about the throat of the bird. "You shall make the small fire for me. Or I will wring your neck before your sisters can find you."

"I do not know the secret myself! The other ones always make the red fire. Oh, do let me go!" The little mud hen was weeping.

"That is a lie! Your sisters commanded you not to tell. So you must know the magic secret. Tell me or I'll choke you." Kokoa's fingers were tighter now about the throat of the bird.

"Oh, I will tell. You are hurting me!" the poor mud hen whispered. "You must have two dry pieces of wood. Take one stick of soft hau wood. Then take a large piece of taro stem. Rub the two together and the red fire will come."

Kokoa held the mud hen fast between his strong knees. He picked up a big taro stem. He found a stick of soft wood in the fire's ashes. Then he rubbed the wood down the taro stem.

Of course, no fire came. There was only a deep groove cut in the taro stem. And the wet taro juice ran from it down on the ground.

"You have lied once again!" Kokoa cried to the mud hen. "Tell me the true magic or I'll choke it out of you."

"It should have been a banana stem. Rub the banana stem with the stick of wood." The mud hen could scarcely speak. Her words came in a whisper.

Kokoa stripped a great green banana leaf off its giant stem. He ran the stick of wood along it. But, of course, there was no fire. The little mud hen was trying her hardest not to tell the magic secret of making fire.

Now the boy truly was angry.

"Tell me the true secret at once!" he cried, and he began to twist the neck of the poor bird. He shook her until it was as if she was in the midst of a sudden typhoon. Almost with her last breath, she gasped, "It is the ohia wood rubbed up on hau wood."

The hau wood is soft, but the ohia is hard, oh, very hard. No other tree of the forests of that island has wood so hard as the ohia.

Kokoa picked up an ohia stick which the birds had left behind them. He rubbed it well against the soft hau wood, and a tiny wisp of smoke came. Then there was a red flame.

"Blow on it, Boy!" the bird whispered. Then the flame grew bigger.

"At last, the fire magic!" Kokoa cried aloud. "I, Kokoa, have learned it for my people."

Kokoa tried making fire once again, then another time. He even put a potato in the hot ashes. For the first time in his life he tasted food cooked on a fire which he had made himself.

You would think that lucky boy would have been satisfied. He had succeeded where all the others had failed. He would have a fine reward.

But he was still angry with the mud hen, who had twice lied to him. And he laid the end of a red-hot stick on top of the bird's head.

That is why, people used to say long ago, this mud hen ever after has had such a red head. This story, too, explains why the stems of taro and banana plants have deep grooves along them.

THE HEAVENLY LOVERS

The world was not always just as it is today. When it was new, strange things took place, so people say. They can scarcely be believed now. But the old tales declare it was so. And what harm does it do for us to hear about them?

This ancient story comes from the land of the Thai people, which once was known the world over as Siam. In those long-ago times the sky was low, so low that a man could leap from the treetops into the heavens. It was much later that the trees and the mountains grew taller and pushed the sky far up over our heads.

At first there was day. And there was night. And then there

came a time when there was only day and no night. This story tells how this came about.

The King of the Sky was, of course, the Sun. Once every day he rode across the heavens in his shining gold chariot, drawn by splendid galloping steeds. Everyone, then, worshiped the Sun King, for he made the day bright, and he gave warmth which the people and plants needed to grow.

When it was time for sleeping, the God of the Sky stabled his horses. He went into his heavenly palace, out of the sight of men. Light was gone from the earth, and there were only the stars, winking and blinking their eyes. They gave a soft light in case anyone needed to go abroad in the night. You see, this was before the bright moon had been hung in its place in the sky.

That was a golden time. There was friendship and peace all over the earth. The King of Siam—which is to say, of all the world—and the King of the Sky were just like two brothers. Flowers bloomed. Fruit ripened. Rice plants covered the land so that everyone had plenty to eat. No one was ever sick, and people were happy.

One day it was made known that the Queen of the Earth, the King's principal wife, was to have a child.

The soothsayers read the stars, and they reported to the people like this: "The royal child will be a girl. A girl child, so fair that no other in the world will compare with her. As beautiful as the dawn she will be."

"Vela Chow" was the way the star readers said it. And Vela Chow, or Beautiful Dawn, was the name which was given the baby Princess, even before she came into the world.

It was as the soothsayers foretold it. No other girl in this

ancient world had such shining beauty. And with each year of
her life she grew more fair.

When she was sixteen years old, people said, "Our Vela Chow
is now old enough to be married. But who on the earth would
be worthy of her?" Everyone loved the girl. Wherever she
went, it seemed that the flowers were brighter and the birds
sang more sweetly.

One day as Vela Chow walked across a green meadow to
the banks of a stream a band of bright butterflies flew round
her head. One huge golden creature brushed her smooth
cheek, then danced in the air before her eyes.

Vela Chow reached out to catch the shimmering yellow butterfly. But, with a quick flash of its golden wings, it flew out of
her reach.

That was a pretty race, between the girl and the butterfly.
Vela Chow ran this way and that, with her fair face turned
upward toward the blue sky. That's how it was that the Sun
King, riding over her head in the sky, saw her and straightway
fell in love with her.

The Sun King liked to ride low, close to the land, so that he
might watch over his friend, the King of the Earth. On this
day, he drove his heavenly horses even closer. When it was
time for the Sun to go back into his sky palace so that it would
be night, he did not turn his horses about. He could not bear
to lose sight of the daughter of the Earth King. So he kept
riding and riding, around and around overhead. And there was
no night.

The dark never came now. In the constant warmth of the
sun, flowers and fruits grew twice as fast and twice as big.
The earth people had to try to rest in its bright light. The stars

could no longer shine, for in the bright sunlight their twinkling lights could not be seen.

"Why does our Sky King no longer take his evening rest inside his palace?" the stars asked each other.

The answer was not hard to find.

"Vela Chow, the fair daughter of the Earth King, is the cause of the Sun's madness." This was the report that the spies who were sent to the earth brought back. "The girl is truly like a beautiful dawn, and she is beloved by all. The Sun follows the Earth Princess wherever she goes. He does not let her out of his sight."

This was true. With love in his heart for her, the Sky King watched Vela Chow while she ran after the butterflies, while she sang with the birds, and when she played in the clear waters of the mountain pools. Only one day, when she ran out of the bright sunshine to rest in a dark cave, did he lose sight of her.

In trying to find her again, the Sun King drove his golden chariot down onto the earth itself. He tied his shining steeds to a tree at the mouth of the cave while he went in to find her.

Inside the cave, the Sun wooed Vela Chow with loving words. So bright was his glory, and so shining his face, that she gladly consented to be his bride.

The stars, keeping watch, saw the golden chariot and the Sun's horses standing there at the mouth of the cave. Quickly they sped down to the earth. And they drove the golden chariot far, far away to a good hiding place.

With glee, the stars saw the sky become dark once more. Now their blinking and winking lights could again be seen in the night sky.

When the Sun at last led his young bride out of the cave,

he meant to take her with him up to his sky palace. But no golden chariot was waiting. No shining steeds were to be seen. How should he manage to get back to his kingdom again?

Hand in hand, the Sun and his bride climbed up the tall mountains. They hoped that they could leap from some peak up into the sky. But it was not possible. The trees and the hills had pushed the blue dome far above their heads.

Tears rolled from the eyes of the Sun King. With his golden glory, it does not seem strange that these teardrops fell to the ground as nuggets of gold and buried themselves in the earth.

The mountains themselves took pity upon the Sun in his sadness. They showed him one certain very high peak which rose higher than any other. It was so high, indeed, that the Sun could jump from its top right into his own palace. He held his arms out toward his bride, but, alas, Vela Chow was not strong enough to make such a great leap.

"I will come for you in my golden chariot, my dear One," he called to her. "Soon I will bring you to me here in the sky."

Now it was the turn of Vela Chow to weep. And, lo, her tears became silver. In shining white streams they flowed into the earth. Ever after, when men dug gold and silver out of the ground, they remembered this old story of how gold and silver had come from the Sun King and his bride.

How did the Sun get his golden chariot back again? Was he able to rule once more over his kingdom in the sky? Well, it happened like this, so the ancient tale says:

He soon discovered that it was the stars which had hidden away his chariot and his horses. And he went to them with fierce anger burning upon his face.

"Give me back my golden chariot," he commanded. "The

earth is dark now by day as well as by night. It was not meant
to be so by the God-Who-Made-the-World. The earth people
complain. Flowers and fruits do not grow. Birds no longer sing.
Men cannot live without my warmth and my light."

"You shall have your chariot," the stars promised, "but you
must agree never to shine again during the nighttime. You shall
bring your bride to your kingdom, but she shall stay inside your
palace only half of each month. We, too, have come to love her,
and we have named her Queen of our night. No longer shall
she be known as Vela Chow. She is now our Silver Moon.

"During the half of the month when Silver Moon hangs with
us in the heavens, you may look upon her from your palace.
But you may not come near her. That is our bargain. Agree,
and we will bring back your golden chariot and your steeds."

What could the Sun do but agree? So it was that a part of
each month he kept his bride in his own palace. Then there
was no moon. But the other part of the month, she hung, silver
bright, for all to see, in the sky at night.

Most of the time the Sun kept his promise. But now and
again he would long to kiss his dear wife. Then he would come
across the heavens to find her. He would cause a round shadow
to fall over the silvery face of the Moon in what some people
call an eclipse.

"We must remind the Sun of his bargain with the stars," the
people would say at such times. They would beat their gongs.
They would thump on their drums. They would even shoot
off firecrackers. They made as much noise as they could so that
the Sun King surely would hear them.

And always he did hear. Always, in a short time, he remembered his bargain with the stars. And the shadow would go